The Genuine Stories

The Genuine Stories

Fairfield Book Prize

SUSAN SMITH DANIELS

First Edition
Library of Congress Control Number: 2018932690
ISBN: 978-0-89823-375-9
e-ISBN: 978-0-89823-376-6

New Rivers Press is a nonprofit literary press associated with Minnesota State University Moorhead.

Cover and interior design by Hope Pauly
Author photo by Terry Baker Photography
The publication of *The Genuine Stories* is made possible by the generous support of Minnesota State University Moorhead, the Dawson Family Endowment, and other contributors to New Rivers Press.

NRP Staff: Nayt Rundquist, Managing Editor; Kevin Carollo, Editor; Travis Dolence, Director; Thomas Anstadt, Co-Art Director; Trista Conzemius, Co-Art Director
Interns: Trevor Fellows, Laura Grimm, Kendra Johnson, Anna Landsverk, Mikaila Norman, Lauren Phillips, Ashley Thorpe, Cameron Schulz, Rachael Wing.
The Genuine Stories book team:
Olivia Carlson, Mia Duncan, Laura Grimm, Cameron Schulz, April Schwandt

Printed in the USA on acid-free, archival-grade paper.

The Genuine Stories is distributed nationally by Small Press Distribution.

New Rivers Press
c/o MSUM
1104 7ᵗʰ Ave S
Moorhead, MN 56563
www.newriverspress.com

Contents

"In my life, I have been called many things. On the one side: a healer, a goddess, a saint. On the other: a charlatan, a trickster, a witch. I have lived such a long time, so who knows? Perhaps they are all true."

From *There is No Such Thing as Magic: A Memoir* by G. Eriksson

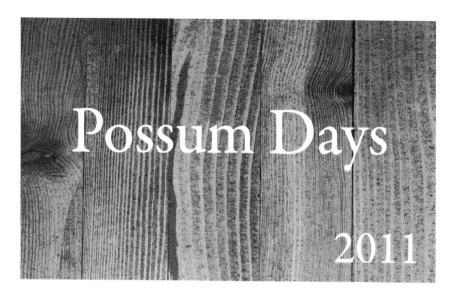

Possum Days

2011

The dead possum was in the bike lane again today, so bloated from the warm weather that I had to swerve into the road.

"Look at him," I called to Kevin and immediately felt the air brush of a passing SUV.

"He's going through a growth phase," Kevin called back.

That was funny for Kevin. And then, of course, "Keep your eyes on the road!"

Kevin the Keeper. He hates it when I take my eyes off the road. He caught up to me where the lane widens a bit before it narrows back down to nearly nothing. This stretch of Via de La Valle has disappearing and reappearing bike lanes, and the SUVs commandeer the road like tanks on a mission. But it's also lovely at this spot, where the road meets the hill and is shaded by the tall eucalyptus trees. I breathe them in. Their fall scent is like tinder reaching toward the sun for a spark. Across the road is a large vegetable farm. I wonder about the possum, if he came out of the field and tried to cross. Did the driver who hit him hear the thud? I can't help but think about these sorts of things.

You may have heard of me. My name is Genuine Eriksson, and I'm kind of famous, which is a sorry fact. I'm a healer. I see sickness and death all the time. I don't work on animals, though, and the possum had been dead for some time.

We're here in California on vacation, where we've been coming for the last five years. We rent the same little cottage every September when the weather is still warm and the traffic to the beach is light because the summer people have all gone back to Arizona, or wherever it is they came from. The owners live in a bigger house on the large orchard property. They are a nice older couple, Lillian and Fred. I healed her some years ago, when we were still traveling to see people. That's how we found out about the cottage. Lillian's doing just fine now, though I wasn't here for Fred's stroke.

◇—◇—◇

Finishing the bike ride is the hardest part of our morning routine, peddling the steep half-mile up to the house. We usually start out going into the village, riding the curvy roads with their lyrical Spanish names like Puerto del Sol and Linea del Cielo—Door of the Sun and Line of the Sky. The little Rancho Santa Fe village is fairly level and centered around a charming boulevard with an island of trees and flowering shrubs down the middle. Banks, restaurants, and real estate offices line either side. Ordinary commerce is rare, and even the small fancy food store is out of the way on a back street. We check for mail at our rental box, grab a coffee, or just sit in the park and drink from our water bottles. Kevin and I take turns going in for the mail and to one of three coffee shops. We try not to frequent any one establishment too often and mix up our cycling clothes with jeans or shorts. That way, the weekend spandex brigade will ignore us "amateurs." Since we look a little bit like we don't belong, but not enough like we couldn't belong, we usually just get the "gloss over" from everyone else. That's Kevin's term for the particular kind of look the locals reserve for people outside their own important orbits. It works for us.

Our daily stop in the village park has been the venue of recent discussions about our life. It's good to keep these things out in the open, away from the confinement of the closed doors of the cottage, where words tend to hang in the air like dust that won't settle.

Yesterday, Kevin said, "Gen, I'm not getting any younger."

Kevin is nearing fifty, and I am the age he was when I healed him of testicular cancer fifteen years ago. He swooped me into his life out of a jumble of relief, gratitude, and zealous and jealous love. I had gratitude of my own—being out from under the careful protection and triangular tension of my family and that wild-eyed priest, Father Hanson, who thought I was going to be his ticket to Rome. Kevin was tall and lean, handsome (still is) with wavy brown hair given to summer highlights, although it's starting to gray around the temples. This life is getting to him. This is not a new conversation.

"You know I can take care of you until you're quite old."

I fluttered my hands in a gesture we're both used to. It's a kind of shorthand between us, a private joke for what I do. We were sitting on a bench overlooking the boulevard, empty on a sleepy Monday, the restaurants closed.

"That's not what I'm talking about," he said, his brow furrowed.

I knew this. I tucked my hands under my legs and gave him my attention. He's looking for immortality of another kind. Children. He's looking for normalcy. Marriage. Life without healing. An ordinary life.

For the last several years we've been living, hiding out really, in the Smoky Mountains of North Carolina. The media had been pursuing me, and people from everywhere hounded us sometimes just to get rid of a cold that was gone by the time they found our door. I'm not saying I can heal everyone, but I'm pretty good at it. We had to move a couple of times at first, but I'm content enough where we are now—down a hard-to-find road and up a hard-to-find driveway. It's mostly only the very sick who find us, and Kevin manages all of that. When he first talked about wanting a normal life, we started coming here for vacations, which used to settle him down.

"Gen, I want us to move here. We've got plenty of money to start over, and even after all these years, no one here knows us. I could go back to work."

Kevin was a software engineer when I first met him.

"Someone is bound to find us," I said. "You know what will happen."

He stood up and started what I call his "walk and talk," pacing this crazy zigzag in front of me, like restless legs syndrome while standing up. He does this when he's got something to say that he thinks I'll resist. Since he doesn't want to lord his full height over my reduced sitting stature, he walks. And talks. And doesn't really go anywhere except back and forth in front of me.

"No, Gen, look at how well it's worked here. We could change our names. Buy a house at the top of one of those long driveways you like so much."

I am in awe of those driveways that seem to go up and up, especially because they have never seen snow or ice. We'd have to cash out everything for a small place here, but that isn't what worries me. I am Genuine the Healer, a fact as plain and undeniable as the sun that rises every day and sets every night.

"I will think about it, I promise," I said to Kevin, knowing that we had another week in California, where he'd been happy. I was happy, and I thought we should just enjoy our one untouchable month—no healing, just rest and relaxation.

After our morning stop, with the mail in my saddlebag, we usually ride down out of the village to the bottom of the hills, around all of the semi-flat, curvy roads and back up that long climb to the house. I like to ride at least an hour. Some days, when Kevin is willing, we cycle all the way to the beach. Those are my favorite rides, although they are damned hard. My heart pounds like I'm pushing to the edge of my own mortality. But I don't say that to Kevin, or I'd never see the seat of my bike again.

After the possum, as we rode back up the hill, the chain came off my bike. We were grinding around one of those blind curves where people put mirrors outside of their driveways. The properties here are bound by tall, flowering hedges with landscaped shoulders up to the edge of the street, and the road traffic is usually light. Kevin pulled up, and I held his bike while he fixed mine. I was next to the curb, drawing in the scent of eucalyptus overlaid with jasmine and gardenia, listening to the weekday sounds of lawnmowers, hammers, and mariachi—all a proper joy for the senses. Hypnotic. I could almost imagine a life here.

I didn't hear the car coming up the hill—an SUV, one of the silver ones. There are only two colors of cars that people seem to buy here: silver or black. And they're always driving too fast. I'm not sure what the hurry is or what those extra five seconds in one's day will buy, because really, on winding, hilly roads like these, you can't save much time by driving any faster than is sensible.

The car swerved and stopped; the screech and the thud were on top of each other the way thunder is to lightning when it's close. I must have jumped back because I fell tangled onto Kevin's bike. He was to my rescue in a flash.

"Are you okay?" In light of our recent discussions, his concern—his "Genuine" concern, as I've always called it—dug a little hole in my heart.

"I'm fine." I stood and brushed off my hands. There was a flurry of hysterical activity.

"Jackson! Oh my God, Jackson!" A pretty blonde woman in a running suit opened the door of the car and partially stepped out. Her hair was in a ponytail, and she looked about thirty something, but it's hard to tell here in California. Looks can be misleading. I peered into the front passenger seat. A boy about eight years old lay unconscious and askew. That must have been the thud. He had on a Chargers T-shirt and jeans, and I could see a faint brush of freckles across his nose. He had the most beautiful blond curls.

"Kevin, call 911." I opened the passenger-side door and told the woman, "My friend is calling for help."

Here, I thought, was part of our problem, Kevin's and mine. What are the words we choose to describe us? Friends? Lovers? Partners? They're all inadequate. Would it make him happy if I could say, "My husband is calling for help"? For a little while, perhaps.

From outside her open door, the woman thrust her head in to shout at me across the seat, "What were you doing there on the side of the road? This is your fault!" Then she sobbed and whispered, "Oh my God. Jackson, wake up. Oh my God. Please, for Mommy. Please, Jackson!"

I didn't bother to ask why he wasn't wearing a seat belt. Or why he was in the front seat. That the airbag hadn't deployed also held a question mark in my mind. That she'd been driving too fast and Kevin and I had been well over on the side of the road was not in question. But I didn't say that, or that she should've checked the round mirror before the bend. Or that she shouldn't have been talking on the phone, since I noticed the Bluetooth in her ear. None of it would have helped the boy, who was getting paler by the second.

Kevin walked toward the car, giving me that look—that "don't do it" look. If I healed this boy, we would have to cut and run and never come back. The word would be out. "Exclusive breaking news here on Fox. Today, in Rancho Santa Fe, California, Genuine Eriksson, the nation's famous reclusive healer, who was known to have been in hiding in the hills of North Carolina, healed a dying boy. Stay tuned for the full story." They would run every old clip they had of me, plus all those dreadful interviews with tangential family members or teachers, and supposed school chums who, as adults, seemed to forget that they were the ones who had picked on me in the school-yard. There would be those quickly-put-together interviews of some of the people I have healed, though for the most part, people were grateful enough to stay quiet, which I always ask of them. They would start in on Kevin and his role as my Svengali, as they liked to call him.

They'd talk about how he met me, our age difference, how he handled my appointments and money and all. And because I never answered questions about Kevin, speculation would explode wilder than a pack of coyotes on a turkey farm. Again.

"Gen, don't," Kevin said in his most quiet, desperate voice. "Please." He wasn't pleading with me to not heal the boy; he was pleading with me to not ruin our life. True, they might be one and the same, but I want to give Kevin some credit. The boy wasn't on his mind—we were on his mind.

There was the tiniest bead of blood on the boy's head, seeping out through his blond curls. If I healed him, I'd have to be sure to wipe that off. There was no decision here. I can't not heal someone. Kevin knew this, too. But for his sake, my mind was racing toward the aftermath and how we might avoid it.

I reached my hand toward the boy's head. His mother screamed, "Don't touch him! Get out of my car!" I heard sirens in the distance and knew I'd have to be quick.

At minimum, I needed to get at least one hand within a foot or so, although that kind of healing takes some extra effort on my part, so really, getting a hand on his head was critical. Touch works best.

"Kevin."

"Gen, please."

"It's all right, Kevin. It will all be all right. Talk to her."

Kevin gave me one of his keeper looks, and there was something else there, too. But he went to the driver's side of the car, where the mother was reaching in for her son.

"Ma'am," he said.

The mother turned around just long enough for me to touch the boy's head. Such pretty curls. I'd almost lost him. I closed my eyes and did my work. I could hear the mother yelling, Kevin trying to soothe her, and the sirens nearing, but I was beyond disturbing. It was just Jackson and me and all that healing warmth and light coursing through me to him and back. I live for this, too.

◇——◇——◇

A little while later, the boy was sitting on a gurney while one para-medic checked his vitals. He turned to the other paramedic and said, "He seems fine. He's alert and knows who and where he is. He even knows who won the game last night. No cuts or bruises, no pain, no apparent head trauma."

The second paramedic was having a conversation of his own. "Ma'am, calm down. Your boy seems fine. He was belted in, so he couldn't have hit his head. There are no signs of any cuts or bruising either. The airbag didn't even deploy. Which is fortunate, because he really would have been hurt."

The mother's face was red and wet and streaked with makeup, and the prettiness seemed to have gone somewhere else. Though on the verge of more hysteria, at the word *belted* she turned sharply toward me. A little too sharply. I gave her a steady, noncommittal look.

The ambulance driver interviewed Kevin over by the bikes. I heard "vacation," "didn't see much," and "overreacting." He said we were staying at the Holiday Inn down by the beach. He gave his name as Frank Jones, and I was, apparently, Mary Jones. I wondered if these were the names he'd picked out for us for the new life he wanted. I wasn't sure we needed the subterfuge just then, but Kevin was always thinking ahead.

I readjusted my helmet and sunglasses and looked at Jackson sit-ting on the gurney, sucking a lollipop. The mother stood by with the two medics, one perched next to the boy.

"Jackson, honey, you were unconscious," she said, her voice still shrill.

The boy looked at his mother, cocked his head to one side, and said, "I don't think I was."

The medic on the gurney patted Jackson's shoulder and said qui-etly to the mother, "Perhaps he was just pretending, playing possum."

The boy smiled, the timid smile of a child who knows he might have unknowingly done something wrong. That's the timid part, and the smile part is the certainty that his parent is in one of those moods that no matter what, she will not be mad at him. It's these times when a child might take whatever irresistible advantage he can. I could see a more thoughtful look around his eyes, that he was sensing this wasn't the time for that. I looked at his head. His curls were a bit sticky, but there was no blood. My hand was sticky, too.

"Jackson?" the mother asked.

The boy shrugged and looked down at his legs, swinging front to back, catching the gurney frame. Little thuds. Thud, thud. He looked at me, at the others, and then at his mother.

"Can we go home now?"

"After we go to the hospital," she said.

When they'd all left, Kevin said to me, "Why did you put the seat belt back on? She was totally negligent. That boy could have died." There was no anger in his voice, just a tired curiosity.

"He nearly did. I did that for us. Belted in, there'd be no reason to believe there was an injury. Without the seat belt, she would have been in a lot of trouble. She won't say anything."

"Ah, Gen. The optimistic healer." There was no smile on his face or irony in his voice, no hopeful ring to optimistic.

"I wouldn't do much good as a pessimistic healer." I smiled to lighten his mood. But I knew what was coming.

"I didn't mean it that way. You're just too optimistic about people." And here his tone felt both flat and accusatory. "After a day or two, that woman's going to get angry that she can't explain what happened." He strapped on his helmet. "She won't tell her husband right away, but she'll keep bugging the boy about it until the husband notices. Then he'll worry about her sanity, and she'll fume and fuss because of him. She'll be all over the Internet. She'll find out. We have to leave tomorrow." He spoke with a weariness worthy of a centenarian who just wants his body to give up, yet wakes every morning to find himself still there, aches and all, stuck in a life that will never get to its destination.

He turned from me and got on his bike and began the slow low-gear ride up the hill toward the cottage.

"Kevin, wait," I called, but he kept cycling, going up that hill the way we both had done every day during the month of September.

The Philosophy of Parenting
1977 - 1982

"Don't move!" the doctor said, for the third or fourth time.

"I'm trying!" Sheila's auburn hair was a mass of sweat-soaked ringlets. She'd been sitting curled over her swollen belly, but as each contraction came she'd straighten up in resistance, and the anesthesiologist had to back away lest he plunge the long needle into the wrong place in her spine. It had been going on like this far too long for either of them.

"Well, it's not good enough," he said. Then, shouting, "Try harder!" He, too, was sweating—small drops around the edges of his scrub cap.

There came a growl from somewhere low and deep, like a string played next to the bridge on a double bass. She didn't seem to be aware she'd made it. Then her hand came up in a perfect arc, fisted and sightless, riding above the perched hypodermic and landed squarely on the jaw of the doctor behind her.

There was commotion and noise, cries from the nurses. Bo, who'd been whispering encouragement to his wife, was jolted out of his solicitude. He dropped his wife's hand and jumped back. "Sheila!"

"Goddammit," the doctor said and put down his instruments. "Lay her down on her side, and bring her knees up."

Ten minutes later, the epidural was done. The doctor left the room without looking at Sheila. A couple of nurses busied themselves around the abandoned tray of instruments. A bottle of fluid hung on a pole with tubing that looped over the rail of the bed and disappeared into the back of her hospital gown. The room was quiet now.

"Sheila," Bo said. "You hit the doctor." He was a young man, tall and thin and fine-featured, with pale eyes and hair.

"He's a sadistic asshole. I asked him to let me lie down in the first place, but he said he couldn't do it that way. Well, guess what? He could." She scanned his face for a reaction and saw the crease of tension in his forehead and a momentary pause in his breathing. He wasn't given to expletives; it wasn't his style. Although he would never criticize her for her own use, she knew it made a discordant pitch, so when she could, she refrained. Not today.

She smiled and pulled him by his arm until he had to sit on the bed. "But I forgive you, Bo, and I feel much better now, too."

He laughed. "Oh, you forgive me, do you? What did I do?" He knew, of course. He smoothed the hospital gown over her swollen belly, then brushed his hand over her brow. The sweat was gone. "Maybe the baby will come faster now."

"Hmm." She lay back on the pillow and caressed the back of his hand. Above her head were clouds painted on a blue ceiling. They were poorly done, and the narrow metal bed and wheeled stands of medical equipment merely underscored the failed attempt at hominess. It jangled with her expectations, some dreamy version of an idyllic and painless experience at home. It was the first of many detours away from their philosophical ideals. Insurance paid for hospital births, not midwives and home births.

A couple of hours later, there was more yelling, this time words of encouragement. "Push, push," and "That's it," and "Good girl," and "Now push again." There was grunting and other deeper, more guttural sounds. Sheila's face went from red to purple and back to red and then pale.

Then a wailing, primordial and high-pitched, and words that buzzed in circles around the room. "Here she is," "Look at her. She's beautiful," and "Look at all that black hair." It was the dominant feature—there was so much of it, and so long and thick for an infant. And black. Deep velvety blue-black.

Once swaddled and quiet, the infant took in her surroundings, peering from dark almond-shaped eyes. The chatter had stalled; glances swarmed back and forth among the staff, looking at the fair young man and the woman with the ruddy curls. Furtive gazes landed on the baby, and then to each parent and back.

"Lots of babies have dark hair that eventually falls out and comes in lighter," offered an aide who had come in to clean up the room. The parents ignored her.

"So it's Genevieve," Sheila said. They'd had other choices, too, for a boy. She held the baby wrapped tight like a lozenge. She touched the edges of the baby's hair as if it were fragile and breakable.

"Genevieve," Bo said, looking only at the hair.

◇—◇—◇

Sheila approached parenting with a vigorous desire to erase the ineptitude of the previous generation's methodologies, which she felt had lacked any designed attempt to improve on the past. That she and all the other baby boomers had been suckled (or more likely, bottled) by parents whose only desire had been to look away from their war-damaged psyches toward the bright middle-class prospects of the future was lost, for the most part, in personal recollections of inadequate attention, missing sensitivities, and inappropriate methods of discipline.

She had been raised by Irish-Catholic parents whose seemingly simple goals had been to have well-behaved children to show off at Sunday mass, older children to mind the younger, and enough children to avoid sideways looks from the nuns and clergy who taught them. That there might be more meat in that nutshell was something Sheila didn't examine often, until much later, when her own parenting experience presented some stupefying obstacles to the perfection she sought.

Bo came from Swedish-Lutheran stock, and though lapsed for the most part, there remained with his family a chilly reserve that Sheila suspected was only partly a climatic memory in their DNA. There was also the barely submerged animosity toward anything Catholic, no matter that she no longer practiced, and the wholly apparent and mutual dissonance felt when their pale coolness met her fiery will. For Bo's sake, she strived to keep it in check.

However, without their families, Bo and Sheila were two prongs on a tuning fork, adjusting naturally to get the right notes. They were young, in love, and saw their future driven by their newly invented wheel of perfected family life.

Like others in their generation, Sheila and Bo had considered themselves at least hippie-ish but were now, in fact, living in a middle-class neighborhood of similar beige brick houses with large fenced-in yards. It was not the dreamy rural existence Sheila had envisioned when Bo wanted to take a job as an actuary in the Midwest, but now they were parents. The baby had their full attention.

Genevieve had not arrived easily, and now the infant's looks became a dominant focus as relatives came and went from their home. Sheila's mother, a freckled redhead, stayed for three weeks, wearing out both Bo and Sheila with constant, nearly compulsive, references to the child's hair and the possibility of some unknown "black Irish" gene popping up. Bo's parents arrived afterward and stayed, thankfully, only two days. They regarded Genevieve politely and held her as you might an alien—carefully, and without looking too much.

Bo's sister, Evie, with a social ineptitude Sheila was only beginning to grasp, obliquely questioned Genevieve's paternity by stating that the baby had "genuine Oriental hair." Something molten erupted in the edgy, sleep-deprived new mother, who declared that the baby would now be called Genuine. Bo knew enough to not confront Sheila at the moment. By the time they resumed a more harmonious pitch, he'd come to think of the baby as the most singular, and therefore genuine, thing to have happened in his life. Plus, he liked standing up for his wife against his family. The absurd name stuck.

It wasn't that they weren't both curious about some errant hair-color allele. The baby's eyes lost their elliptical shape and over time grew to be large round globes of indigo. But Bo never questioned Sheila about the unspoken possibility, and she never expected him to. Genuine was his, and he knew it.

Genuine grew into her hair, to a point. It grew fast and frustrated her mother's attempts to control and shape it. It also gave the baby, and then toddler, a look of maturity that seemed at times uncanny, as if she were a shrunken ten-year-old. But the dark hair was also striking and complemented the child's looks, which now included thick eyebrows. She had a beautiful, if unusual, countenance.

She behaved as all toddlers did. But in her parents' view, she gave "tantrum" a new definition, although they had no reference beyond a few children from a neighborhood playgroup. Sheila figured that Genuine matched her will for will, and Bo silently agreed. By the time Andrew arrived, Genuine was three and ready for preschool. On her first day, her mother swung back and forth on the pendulum between teary-eyed tenderness and loss, and the mantra of "Not a minute too soon."

By the time Lars arrived, not quite two years after Andrew, Sheila was deft at handling the rock-and-roll rhythm of family life. Rocking the children either literally or figuratively in the deep pocket of parental, particularly maternal, love, and rolling with the quick-jab punches that were provided to all parents when God or nature or whatever malevolent force dealt little karmic pokes to one's progeny. Sheila would be the first to admit that she didn't roll so well. Fevers, ear infections, and the like, she could deal with. Accidents that required a trip to the emergency room, not so well . . . But what chiefly caused her happiness to clunk to a stop was emotional distress experienced by her children, or more specifically, Genuine, since her brothers were too young. It usually involved peers, and both Sheila and Bo knew that the child was, in an ironic way, disadvantaged by her looks and growing intelligence. Just now in kindergarten, she was already reading simple chapter books.

Genuine had played with neighborhood kids since her toddler group. Toy grabbing, toddler furies, and the occasional inept pushing had alerted Sheila to which parents shared her sensibilities for safe play, as well as those whose laissez-faire style might put Genuine in danger—even though the child herself would often be the spark in a conflagration. In time, the play dates dwindled to a few choice friends. Throughout these years, Genuine had been notably more comfortable in her own home with her friends. At first Sheila thought Genuine displayed a natural diffidence in strange situations—an experience (according to her Advisors, a term she used for her collection of child rearing books) normal for her age—but as the child matured, she could see there was also a growing reserve, which reminded her of the way Bo could be at times. What she had taken for aloofness had been, at its roots, something altogether different. Or perhaps not.

"I don't want to ride the bus," Genuine informed her parents after several weeks of kindergarten.

The bus stopped every morning at the corner of the street, two doors from their house, and delivered her back at noon. Sheila had walked Genuine to the bus daily after the first week (when she had driven her to school), infant and toddler in tow, and could see that in time she would be able to watch Genuine walk to the bus from the comfort of her front door. Sheila considered the location of the bus stop a stroke of fortunate proximity, considering the prospect of wrapping and unwrapping toddler and infant once the cold weather arrived.

They were at the dinner table, and Genuine had been what Sheila could only describe as sullen all afternoon, though not forthcoming for any reason until now.

"Why is that, honey?" she said.

"I don't like it."

The simplicity of the answer caused her father to smile. Both parents knew that Genuine would parse her answers from emotion to reason. It was her way. And if there were a five-year-old analysis, they would have to delve to find it. That ferocious toddler tantrums could give way to this cautiously mannered, school-aged temperament alternately baffled and amused her parents.

"Did something happen on the bus?" Sheila heard the subtle rise in her own voice, perhaps fear for all the unknown dangers she felt under her motherly skin.

But Genuine simply said, "It takes too long."

She continued to ride the bus because the alternative would have preempted any kind of routine that Sheila needed to maintain for the new infant. Bo promised, if his schedule allowed, to drive her to school once a week, and this seemed to be a good compromise. Sheila questioned the child about the bus ride for the first week afterward with no appreciable response, and finally Bo suggested that she just leave it alone.

There were days, weeks, and more where Sheila lived a hamster-wheel existence of diapers, meals, laundry, and sleep (in that order) in descending quantities. She adapted to the inadequate sleep well on some days and worse on others. She had had a different life BC: before children. Often, while burping a baby, bandaging knees, or shoving barely folded laundry into the kids' dressers, her thoughts were tugged backward to those precious and unappreciated days in graduate school when her main responsibility was nothing more than a self-engrossing study of beautiful things. That, and her courtship with Bo. She even came to miss her more recent role as a docent at what she used to refer to as the dullest museum in America. It all seemed like a very long time ago. Those were her daydreams.

Her night dreams usually involved a child left at school overnight, a baby forgotten at home alone, or a toddler falling into a bizarrely small mole hole. Things were different for Bo, who was busy and keen and attentive to his work. She felt mindless and fraught.

Then there would be days where Lars literally slept like a baby, Genuine came home skippingly happy from school, and Andrew didn't climb on the refrigerator or perform other death-defying acts of boyhood. Genuine, although still not entirely enamored by her peers, had found an ally in her teacher, Miss Kendricks, a recent grad. It was clear to Sheila after their first parent-teacher conference—when Miss Kendricks gushed about Genuine's advanced capabilities, not to mention (she did a few times) her striking looks—that Genuine had become the teacher's pet, something Sheila had never experienced. She was set to wondering how that would have affected her own childhood, but there was no jealousy, only fulsome warmth as Sheila realized that Genuine's school career was off to a good start.

Every good day has its opposite, Sheila thought, when a call from the school found her sitting in an uncomfortable chair across from an empty desk on a frigid December morning, baby at her feet in his carrier, toddler hurriedly left at a neighbor's. She was waiting for the principal, Mr. Atkinson, to arrive.

The office had two windows. The one to the front of the school had a view of diminished patches of dirty, icy snow spread across a dull khaki lawn, like leftover platters at a meal, and a single tall evergreen standing in no particular place, like the last invited guest who didn't know where to sit. December in Iowa could be bleak, Sheila thought. The other window framed the larger bustling office, through which everyone reached the principal. It was noisy on the other side of the glass. Boisterous children could be heard in the hall beyond, someone was making announcements on the PA system, phones rang, and file cabinets slammed. Lars, who had slept through the cold walk from the car, began to stir.

"Has Genevieve complained about the bus?" Mr. Atkinson, bespectacled, sixty-plus, and appearing put-out, was now sitting across from Sheila. He looked at his desk and let out an almost imperceptible sigh.

A few weeks after Genuine's initial complaint about riding the bus, she'd been more adamant. "I'm not riding the bus again."

She was also more forthcoming. Apparently some older boys had been commenting on Genuine's thick eyebrows, and had been for some time. Sheila knew that at five, it was probably impossible to ignore. As she thought about it more, she realized it would be hard to ignore at any age. She made a note to herself to check in with her Advisors for counsel.

"Genuine, honey, Mommy can't drive you to school every day. Not with the baby," Bo had said at dinner that night.

"I know it's hurtful when people say things that are mean," Sheila added. "It happens, and it's hard to ignore."

"I'm not grouchy," Genuine said.

"Did they say you were grouchy?" Bo asked.

"Well, they called me Groucho." Sheila and Bo glanced at each other and then away, so as not to appear amused. Sheila wondered which child had been watching old Marx Brothers' movies. Or had one heard a parent refer to Genuine this way? The fact was, Genuine's eyebrows didn't really look like Groucho's; they were more like Frida Kahlo's, scurrying to the inside to meet each other, particularly in moments like these when she was perturbed.

"I can't drive her to school every day, and I don't think we should anyway," Bo said after the children had all gone to bed. But he did drive her to school for a week. Sheila had then walked her to the bus for the following week, toddler and infant wrapped for the weather. She glowered through the bus windows at whichever child was watching, just in case someone in there had an idea to continue the torment.

Sheila looked past the principal to the scene beyond the window. It had begun to snow. "She told us that some children were calling her names. It was about her eyebrows."

They had decided, in what Sheila had privately, resentfully, thought was a 60:40 decision, that allowing Genuine to learn to cope with the teasing was the best solution. Sheila would not, as Evie had suggested when Genuine was three, "take a tweezers to those things."

Genuine needed to learn by living, Bo had said. Name-calling was a part of childhood. It would make her stronger. Sheila and Bo's relationship devolved to this—she the worrier, he the cool-headed logistician. Of course, that's who they had always been, but having children seemed to eliminate other parts of their past selves, the ones who would meet each other in the middle, the ones who could forget morning spats before the coffee got cold. And certainly, the vision of their children growing up in some mythically perfect world of their creation was long in the past.

Sheila thought that whatever was happening now certainly had to involve more aggressive behavior than name-calling. She was trying hard not to be alarmed, or at least not to appear alarmed.

"Well, I don't know about that part. The thing is, and I'm really sorry, but . . ." Mr. Atkinson proffered a manila envelope across the desk. Sheila had to rise up out of her chair to take it; such was the depth of his desk. The envelope was unsealed, and she could quickly see what was in it. She felt faint, and at that moment, Lars started to fuss from his carrier on the floor, raising decibels by the second. It really was a world to wail in, she thought, as she clutched two lengths of amputated braids.

"Let me see her," came out in a kind of breathless croak. She felt subsumed in a dizzying torrent of questions that she could not articulate . . . who, how, when? Scissors? Terror? She unbuckled the now screaming baby and bounced him while clutching the braids, only just noticing that the principal had left the room. She reached for the desk phone and called Bo at work. "You need to come home," was all she could say.

Genuine came into the office with the principal. Her hair, which required daily restraint, now billowed above her shoulders like de-polarized magnetic fibers. Suddenly, the blackness of it all struck Sheila. She felt the dark dagger of conscience. She had failed to protect her child.

"Where's her coat?" It was the only logical question left to ask. The other details didn't matter; getting the child away from the school did.

"We need to talk about some other things, Mrs. Eriksson. There was some damage on both sides."

Sheila looked at the principal as if he were an odd piece of abstract art that she could not decipher. "Where's her coat?" she asked again, raising her voice above Lars, who had been momentarily mollified but was now screaming at full pitch while she strapped him back into the carrier.

She didn't wait for a response, but instead led Genuine by the hand to her classroom door. With the baby carrier slung through to her elbow, she realized she was still clutching the braids and had yet to say anything to the child. She drew the child to her in what she hoped, above Lars's screams, would be an informative, if wordless, hug: that she was safe now with her mother, that nothing like this would ever happen again, and that her mother was sorry, so very sorry that she hadn't heeded the warnings, those previously obscure warnings, which now, in entirely unexamined retrospect, seemed all too clear.

"Go inside, honey, and get your coat. We're going home."

"What about Miss Kendricks?" This question confirmed Sheila's opinion that her unwary child, still thoughtful in the face of what she had experienced today, was a paragon of innocence in a noisy, bullying world.

Later, Bo would resist his wife's overarching and negative view of elementary school life as it related to their daughter. The name-calling, which had gone on for some time, was not a one-way experience. Genuine, when questioned by Bo, admitted to slinging a few verbal stones herself. He wasn't sure where she had learned "Cro-Magnon" and was less sure, after a school-organized meeting with the boy and his parents that the boy would have understood more than its tonal intentionality. The fact that Genuine had struck back, literally, with her metal lunch box, cutting the boy's forehead, disturbed Bo more deeply than Genuine's shorn locks. He had felt that he and Sheila adhered deeply to a non-violent approach both to conflict and child-rearing. He would have resisted the draft if he hadn't drawn a lucky number in the lottery.

The boy's parents were also upset, although to be reasonable, he had brought scissors and deliberation to the deed. And the boy was so much bigger than Genuine. Sheila saw surprise in their faces when shown the shocking pieces of braided evidence. In the end, there were no school sanctions for students so young. The children were made to apologize to one another.

Bo was pleased that Genuine did not seem overly traumatized by the event, and he looked forward to things going back to the way they had been. He did take to inserting, during Genuine's bedtime routine in which he read to her and she read to him, lengthy discussions on the value of non-violence, tailored, he felt, to her five-year-old understanding.

Sheila, on the other hand, became anxiety-ridden about the "what ifs" of the violence—the tit for tat that had not taken place. The possibility of retaliation with scissors in hand kept her drummed up for weeks. She channeled her anxious energies into looking at educational alternatives. Homeschooling was out due to the evolving needs of the younger siblings, leaving few options.

"There is no way we're sending her to a private school, let alone a religious school." Bo was cool and adamant when Sheila presented him with the only alternatives to public schooling. Truth was, private school was against their philosophy of parenting. In graduate school, it had been a "topic" between them. Sheila had attended Catholic school and had not wished to burden any of her children with the experience. Bo had done well in public school, and it suited his egalitarian approach to life, in addition to his careful sense of economy.

"We have to do something." Sheila felt like she was speaking to the air.

And so began another phase in the life of Bo and Sheila Eriksson. Though Genuine seemed happy enough in school, Sheila remained hyper-vigilant for further signs of torment. Bo had to repeatedly remind her that her attention on what might happen could turn Genuine into an anxious child, though there were no signs of that yet. Genuine had actually asked to return to the bus. Sheila's anxiety had been further fueled by more sleepless, teething-baby nights and the start-and-stop routine of making separate trips to deposit and retrieve Genuine and Andrew—now in preschool—from their different locales with their dissimilar schedules. This was not lost on Bo. He was a doting father with a pragmatic nature. If Genuine wanted to ride the bus, that was good enough for him. If he could fulfill her desire and stone the other bird of Sheila's frantic schedule, one that fed her increasingly fractious temper, so much the better. While he could not imagine life without Genuine (and the boys to a lesser degree), he, too, occasionally longed for BC times when all of this family life was a theoretical fantasy that he and Sheila had planned over quiet dinners with wine.

However, it was three months before Sheila agreed to allow Genuine to ride the bus again. And she didn't so much agree as relinquish her authority on this point to Bo.

"Genuine, honey, how would you like to start taking the bus again tomorrow?" Bo asked at dinner one spring night.

He had not discussed this with Sheila. At least, he had not discussed it in the past few days. Her answer had always been no. But at the end of a long, long day, Sheila was too tired to find her voice of objection.

"Sure," Genuine said. She cast a worried glance at her mother. Sheila heard a voice coming through a long tunnel of her tired brain, a voice of reasonableness that she'd not heard in many months. It said something like this: The child is now worrying about you. You're tired. Get a grip. Let it go. Bo's right; she'll be fine. You have three children, not just one. Sheila saw Bo and Genuine looking at her in wait.

"Whatever you say," she said to Bo.

So Genuine began to ride the bus again. She remained cheerful, and even convinced her mother to let her walk to the bus alone. She started having friends home after school. They would disappear into her bedroom for the whole afternoon if Sheila let them, but she wouldn't. She checked on them and devised breaks for snacks or activities at the kitchen table. The girls would participate for a while, then scamper back to Genuine's room. Sheila could hear them giggling and laughing. She was pleased that Genuine was getting to be more social, but she also had some nagging feeling about this sudden change in behavior. Bo thought Sheila was over-thinking again. Life seemed so simple to him. If you couldn't see ripples, why worry about the monster at the bottom of the lake?

◦–◇–◦

It was the Barbies. Genuine came home from a birthday party with Barbie and Ken in tow. Sheila found herself stumped for a way to respond. It wasn't that Genuine hadn't asked for a Barbie in the past; she had, and her parents had declined. Bo had thought it wasn't a big issue, but he went along with Sheila's impassioned view that Barbie, with her unusual anatomy and pea-sized head, was not an appropriate role model for their daughter of unusual looks and distinctive intelligence. There was the other side of the argument: the more you deny the child something she wants, the more attention she will put on it, until it becomes a colossal something in her awareness. Though vigilant for a burgeoning obsession, Sheila had yet to see evidence.

"Genuine, honey, whose Barbies are those?" Sheila asked after giving herself a minute to recover and recalculate.

"They're mine." The child looked at her mother as if it was the most natural thing to be proudly holding these two previously forbidden fruits.

"Sarah got three sets for her birthday, so she gave these to me." And then quickly, as a defense to a yet unmounted offense, "It's okay because they were a gift. And only one is a Barbie. The other is Ken."

Checkmate, Sheila thought. Bo should teach her chess. She'd be beating him in no time. This thought warmed Sheila just a bit, which also made her feel guilty. But here was the evidence, and the child had found a way to procure the dolls.

"Okay, honey. You can have them. But just these two. We aren't buying any others."

Bo was amused that evening as Genuine displayed the dolls for him. Later, he and Sheila laughed at the child's maneuvers and felt happy they were at last sharing some common ground. It felt good. It felt like old times.

Sheila still occasionally wondered whether a change in schools might be a good idea. She often took Lars on a walk past the Catholic school two blocks away. She watched the children in the playground and considered whether or not the children looked relaxed, carefree, and not overly constrained. She decided they did. But the issue had died in the primary, and she wasn't willing to raise another campaign. Kindergarten was almost over, and the kids would be home all summer. She looked forward to all-day school for Genuine in the fall.

When Lars could go a few hours without nursing, Bo offered to babysit so Sheila could have Saturday afternoons to herself. This was a routine harking back to pre-Lars days when Bo would take the two older children for part of every Saturday so Sheila could rest or catch up on housework or just sit staring at the wall. With three kids and Lars still so young, it worked better if Sheila went out and left everyone at home. She took to going to afternoon movies. She watched good movies and terrible movies; it didn't matter. Being surrounded by strangers in a dark theater where no one knew her as "Mama" was an earthly form of heaven.

On a suddenly chilly day in late May, Sheila arrived home from the matinee to an uncommonly perplexed and deflated Bo.

"Is anything wrong? Did someone get hurt?" she asked.

She looked around the family room. Lars was asleep in his swing, head resting on his chest. Andrew was sitting close to the television, watching a barely audible cartoon.

"Where's Genuine?"

"She's in her room."

Sheila saw Barbie and Ken next to Bo on the sofa, all legs in the wrong direction, attached to each other in the wrong place.

"What's with Barbie and Ken?" she laughed.

"They're fucking," Bo said.

"What?" Sheila could not remember when she'd heard Bo use that expression. It was just not part of his vocabulary.

"That's what she said."

"Who?" Sheila said, feeling a bit disoriented after her quiet afternoon at the movies.

"Our five-year-old daughter." And then, "Tell me about those private schools."

The Healer

January 1986

Until that week, Sheila thought that Genuine had been happy at St. Timothy's. Tuesday, she had come home from school obviously upset, eyes furtive and periodically brimming. Sheila did a quick scan for signs of physical injury—it wouldn't be the first time.

"What happened?"

"Nothing." The child pulled away from her mother. "Can I go do my homework now?" Genuine had her own timing for everything, Sheila knew. She let her go.

After the trouble in kindergarten, her parents, despite their agnostic leanings, had transferred her to St. Timothy's, and now she and Andrew both attended the Catholic school.

By dinnertime, Genuine was cheerful. Bo had a (somewhat) engrossing story to tell about his job and the beauty of mathematics. Sheila was engaged in thoughts of a childless stroll through the Louvre. Both interrupted their verbal and nonverbal reveries to remind the children to eat (Andrew), stop throwing food on the floor (Lars), and to quit kicking her brother (Genuine). Sheila forgot to ask Genuine about the school day.

It snowed heavily overnight, leaving the children home the next day. Though the family lived within walking distance of the school, many other children came from farther afield either by school bus or parent. Sheila didn't mind the snow day. It gave her a break in her own routine of packing lunches and trundling Lars off to preschool and back. The two little boys were already out in the backyard, fenced and protected and easy to watch from both the kitchen and the family room.

Sheila was mildly concerned about Genuine, whose face was flushed and warm, a recurring phenomenon of the last week or so, though her temperature remained normal. Still, she kept her inside in case she was on the verge of the flu or something. Flushed or not, her daughter was smiling, sitting by the window with her boots and snow pants on the floor beside her. Her dark braids were nearly long enough to pool in her lap. Her thick eyebrows rose up in a silent plea. Sheila could be occasionally disarmed by the child's looks as much as strangers often seemed to be. Genuine, knowing nothing different, treated the interest as a natural facet of her life. She was brave and curious about the world, though given to moments of intractability with her peers that confused and sometimes alienated them. Sheila wondered again what might have happened at school the previous day.

"I'm fine, Mama," Genuine said. "I feel good. Really good."

And it was true. Sheila could see that. Outside the window, the snowfall abated, and Andrew and Lars were trying to roll a snowman. Genuine looked at her mother with expectation and hope.

"Okay, you can go outside," Sheila said.

The boys, who adored their older sister, were quick to engage her as she stepped out of the house.

There were stretches of time in the lives of their children that rolled along smoothly enough. Sheila and Bo were enjoying one of those times now. The children were in school (though Lars only half-day), self-sufficient enough to dress themselves, rummage the kitchen for food, and talk and play together for at least some period of time—enough for Sheila to have a moment, whatever filled it: a cup of coffee, part of the newspaper, reverie, or daydreaming.

On Thursday, a bright, cold day with winds that promised to plummet the temperatures, Sheila found herself in the principal's office at St. Timothy's. It made her remember the noisy office at the public school. It was more private here, though she wondered if that was a good thing. Sister Dorothy sat anchored behind an enormous glass-topped desk. Sheila saw no sign of finger marks or smudges, just a single pile of papers in front of the nun and three small religious figurines floating on an ocean of spotless glass. It dawned on Sheila, as she puzzled out this tidy island in a school of over two hundred children, that she felt oddly dwarfed and then realized that the height of her chair was lower than the nun's. Was it in deference to the children who would be sitting in the chair, or was it to make a parent less comfortable, less confident? She didn't have time to ponder this further as Sister Dorothy was talking again about Genuine, whom she carefully referred to as Genevieve.

"We know that she is a beautiful child, but we don't like to put attention on that. We don't know why God has given beauty to some and not to others. We know that she is a good student. We also know that Genevieve, despite all of this, is not popular with her peers."

Sheila could see that Sister Dorothy had probably never been pretty. Her eyes were dark and small, and she had a thin but sizeable nose and a small mouth, all set inside a narrow, rectangular frame. The nuns of this order no longer wore their traditional habits, but Sister Dorothy managed to attire herself in such a way that no one would mistake her for a layperson. She kept her salt-and-pepper hair short and pulled back from her forehead under a wide black headband, which accentuated her hawkish features. From what Sheila had observed since the children started at St. Timothy's, Sister Dorothy's clothing palette was a trinity unto itself: black, white, and gray. A large crucifix on a black cord hung around her neck, reaching down to her mid-chest. She was not comforting to look at.

Sheila wanted to interrupt, to insert herself in this conversation at the outset, hold her flag up for Genuine before the nun gained ground, but Sister Dorothy continued.

"Two days ago, Danny Fowler, a student a year above Genevieve, was observed punching students in the schoolyard."

"Was Genuine punched?" Sheila's ire rose as she began to stand.

Again with emphasis on the name, the nun said, "Genevieve and Danny were recruiting students to line up to get punched."

"I don't believe it," Sheila said. She stood and looked down at the nun. She knew well that Genuine could be obstinate, but never willfully mean or unkind.

Sister Dorothy reached up toward her shoulder as if to adjust her sweater, but her hand fell back to the desk before making contact. Sheila wondered if it was an old tic from when the nun wore a wimple.

"I saw it myself," the nun said. "Please sit."

She looked down at her desk, fiddling with some papers until Sheila sat.

"Genevieve was doing something else, too. After Danny hit the children, she laid her hands upon them as if she were healing them."

From her Catholic upbringing, Sheila was familiar with the stories of saints and their miracles, and Christ's healing of the sick and raising of the dead. She breathed in relief. Surely this event was some sort of acting out the kids did in relation to a lesson they were learning in school. She and Bo had appreciated the fact that St. Timothy's required more discipline of its students, thinking it would protect Genuine, but they had regarded these mandatory religion classes as something of a drawback. In time, they hoped, more non-Catholic children would attend the school and more parents would be able to pressure for another option.

Sheila felt the hardness of the chair beneath her and annoyance that she'd been called in for something so silly. She shifted her weight. "Surely, this was just some child's play."

Another feint toward the phantom wimple as the nun said, "Well, yes of course." She put her elbows on the desk and leaned toward

Sheila. "Except that one child sustained a bloody nose, and her parents are quite upset."

Sheila could feel the heat rising in her face and took some deep breaths. Bo was always telling her to do that. The heat never rose in his calm, pale features. He was absolutely stoic in comparison to her. Sheila wondered what he would do if he were sitting here.

"But Genuine didn't actually hurt anyone herself, right?"

Later, after the children were home from school, Sheila tried, with little luck, to talk to Genuine about the incident. In response, Genuine knitted her brows, chewed her lip, and mumbled about homework before heading off to her room. She could be stubbornly patient, or, Sheila thought, maybe it was patiently stubborn. She felt like an explorer, always forging new territory with Genuine. The boys were easier, more predictable. She decided to wait until Bo came home.

That evening, as Genuine's version of Tuesday's event unfolded, Sheila thought of this era with the children and how she would miss it. She hadn't really known it was there—like something she caught a glimpse of in the rearview mirror, and the traffic was now flowing so heavily in one direction that she would never be able to turn around and go back. She also thought of something she had never known: that there is nothing quite as frightening as the realization that your child might either be an inveterate liar or, worse, delusional.

"Someone threw a rock, and it hit Danny Fowler in the face. It started bleeding, so I went up to him and put my hand on him," Genuine said.

"Why would you put your hand on his face if it was bleeding?" Sheila asked.

Bo glanced over and pursed his lips for her to stop. They had agreed that Bo would do the questioning. Bo didn't question the child so much as wait for her to talk. He could definitely match Genuine for patience. Sheila had none.

"I don't know." Genuine shrugged and looked plainly at her father. "I just did." Sheila took deep breaths and tried to manage her tongue.

"Anyway, when I touched his cheek, my hands got really warm. And then the bleeding stopped."

Sister Dorothy hadn't told Sheila this part of the story. Apparently, Danny's wound, if there had been one, had gone away once Genuine put her hand on it. Perhaps this was when the examples from their religious lessons got the boy excited. Danny had claimed Genuine was a healer. He wanted her to try it again. He handed her a rock to throw at him, but she refused. So Danny had grabbed a younger boy and punched him in the face, then made Genuine touch his face, too. The child claimed that Genuine's hand took the pain away.

"I didn't want to do it. I don't like Danny Fowler. But he was hurting those kids, so I had to."

"You had to what, honey?" Bo said.

"I had to fix them."

"How many children were there?" Sheila asked, stepping in again, but Bo didn't seem to mind. The wind rattled through the one window in the living room as it always did this time of year. Sheila was briefly distracted and irritated that another year had passed and it went unfixed. She tried to envision children in the schoolyard in sub-zero temperatures and remembered two days ago the weather had been relatively balmy. Then the snow. Then the wind that brought the arctic temperatures.

Genuine looked at her mother now, and Sheila, with a rising uneasiness, noticed a certain pride as the child said, "Twelve. I even put Lindsay Peterson's tooth back in, and it stayed."

"What?!" Bo said as Sheila collected herself back into the moment.

"Danny punched her right in the mouth. It bled a lot, and her tooth came out. It wasn't a baby tooth either." Genuine looked at her parents, although Sheila could not say what she thought the child expected. Not admonition.

Sheila now found herself desperate to tether this new episode in their lives to anything other than magical thinking or mental illness. Her experience with "unreasonable behavior" was limited to Bo's sister, Evie, whose intensely volatile emotional life resided at the far edge of normal.

Sister Dorothy hadn't mentioned this tooth thing, and Sheila didn't know how to begin unraveling all the parts of what may or may not have happened. She was more concerned with what Genuine believed happened.

"Emily Mays ended up with a bloody nose," Sheila said. She had to push the words past a lump in her throat that tasted a bit like fear.

"That's because I got really tired. It didn't work anymore." Genuine put her palms up and shrugged. "And then the bell rang, and we had to go back in. Danny got really mad and said it was all my fault."

Bo had a bemused smile as he said, "Genuine, honey, you weren't really healing those children. Sometimes people think they feel some way just because someone tells them they should. Particularly if that person is kind of bossy, like Danny."

Sheila wondered where Bo got his calm. What he said made perfect sense, and for a moment, she almost—but not quite—started to think she'd been overreacting.

"No, Daddy," Genuine said. "I did it again after school. Danny made me. He got a pen and jabbed it into the back of his hand until it bled. Then I fixed it. The heat came back, and it worked."

Sheila turned to Bo, who was looking at Genuine with an expression she had never seen before. Check.

"No, really, sweetie. It was just a game."

"No, Daddy. You don't understand. I'm a healer." The child held up her hands, palms forward, in what could be an invitation to play patty-cake.

Bo took Genuine into his lap and stroked her hair, saying, "It was just a game. It was just a game."

Genuine pushed away and got down—tears brimming, brows knitting furiously, arms folded across her chest, staring at her parents. Sheila looked at Bo, who was eyeing his daughter as one might eye an insect under a microscope. The rattling wind had stopped, and the room was quiet deep into its corners. Sheila glanced around and tried to find her bearings in the inanimate objects of their lives: the child-worn sofas, the large trunk-turned-coffee-table her grandmother had brought from Ireland, a wall lined with department store portraits of the kids, their wedding photos, another wall with a few paintings she had done in art class as an undergraduate. There was nothing here that offered her a mooring.

Sheila thought about the strange flushing Genuine had been prone to lately. She sensed that they were now adrift in an unknown world that would include doctors and tests—and possibly psychiatrists and more tests—and on down into a blind tunnel of wrongness. She couldn't look at Bo, and she couldn't look at Genuine. But then Genuine was in her lap, caressing her cheeks.

Sheila felt small—smaller than a pinpoint in a vast universe of unknowns—as the child in her lap appeared large, strange, and alien.

"It's okay, Mama," Genuine said. "I can fix you."

Expectations

May 1987

Bo wondered if all historic events, large and small, began as uneventful days.

During a warm spell in early May, their three kids scrambled for shorts and T-shirts; however, Bo and Sheila knew their enthusiasm didn't quite match reality. It was sixty degrees, not eighty. Nevertheless, there was a joyful buoyancy in the house. Suddenly tall, seven-year-old Andrew donned a pair of turquoise and pink striped shorts, hand-me-downs from his older sister, with unabashed satisfaction. The day had an ease about it that Bo hadn't experienced in some months. He'd suggested to Sheila that she take off by herself for a couple hours, leaving him to hold down the fort. He was keen to be sure that she got time to herself.

"Thanks, but there's too much laundry," she said. "Plus, Heather's coming to babysit tonight, remember?"

Now he did. He could probably dig deeper into his recollection of the week and remember when Sheila had given him notice for whatever she planned for this evening. But he didn't bother.

"Remind me where we're going tonight?"

"The new exhibit opening at the museum."

"Ah. Good."

Sheila gave him a quick glance, checking, he thought, for sarcasm. Or perhaps not.

"I mean it," he said, just to cover his bases. He looked forward to any time he could get his wife out and put her mind on things beyond the children—Genuine in particular.

Sheila smiled. "Good, me too."

In Bo's opinion, when it came to the children, Sheila had a tendency to augment things beyond their significance. When they were young, he attributed this to lack of sleep. But whether it had become habit, or an unfurling of some previously guarded tendency in her he'd not been privy to, it was a fact of life now. Sheila was a woman of high passions mixed with fretful brooding over their children.

Humming, she dithered about from the laundry room to the family room, where she was folding. Bo grabbed for her, pulling her under his shoulder as they faced the backyard, where Genuine, Andrew, and Lars ran, tagged, made triumphal calls of 'you're it,' and ran some more. Proud, happy parents in a moment of sanity. Happy children, happy wife. No small event of late.

"Do you think if we get a picture of Andrew in those shorts, we can blackmail him with it when he's a teenager?"

She swatted him with socks he'd left on the sofa and turned to tidy the family room. It occurred to him that their daughter's experience with the psychiatrist these past several months was having a positive effect on Sheila. Perhaps she'd begun to believe, as he did, that the children had their own destiny, even a day-to-day destiny, events that had to be experienced, no matter how well they were shielded. Or "Sheila'd," as he liked to kid her. For everything they could control, there were exponentially so many more things they could not.

They had been all over it together, again and again.

"We were wrong about the name," Sheila said one night after one of Genuine's early appointments with Dr. Wittstein. "It was a terrible thing to do to a child," she continued, referring to the way they'd continued to call her "Genuine," even after the child started having playmates and then attending school. Sheila felt it had given the child a feeling of undue significance.

"Did Dr. Wittstein say that?"

"No, but we had a discussion about her name today, which was very calculated to not lay blame. You know how he is. 'Just the facts, please.'"

The silly name had stuck through infancy, a special little joke. Bo called her his "Genuine" baby, who "Genuinely" kept them up all night. She was "Genuinely" beautiful. They never tired of it. Later, of course, they reverted to Genevieve, but not before Bo had concocted a nighttime fable for the child about her special "secret" name, which magnified it in the child's mind. Eventually, she would answer to nothing else—even if she were sitting right at the table. It had caused problems in both schools, of course, and particularly at St. Timothy's; she'd had to learn to endure "Genevieve" when called upon. But she never suffered anyone close to her using her Christian name.

Now, odd black hair and all, Genuine clearly had some of Bo's features: his ears, with their attached lobes, not to mention a matching set of feet, small replicas of his long toes and high arches. Her personality was cool like his, too, except for occasional tempestuous outbreaks, but more often she was level-headed and filled with logical arguments for whatever she deemed important. That's what had flummoxed them both so much about the child's fantasy, which, after a time, Sheila insisted on calling a delusion. In private, of course.

Genuine's confidence this past year in her schoolyard healing powers escalated to a belief so strong that Sheila had nearly lost her own sensibilities. It was only in the last month that their daughter had quit insisting on this power, quit trying to prove to them that she could heal people, that she was a "Genuine" healer.

Dr. Wittstein had examined all of these things in minutiae, of course. For this, and other things, Sheila mostly blamed herself. When it came to the children, she felt responsible for all things big and small. Bo, who was happy to be out of the blame orbit, felt that the child would have been just fine without Dr. Wittstein, that

Sheila was hypersensitive about their daughter and lacked perspective. Bo planned to encourage her to go back to work as soon as Lars, age four, was in school all day.

Sheila settled on the sofa to fold laundry. The children were making happy noises outside, and Bo could hear birds singing. He felt as if they had landed from a long time at sea.

$$\diamond\!-\!\Diamond\!-\!\diamond$$

It seemed as if all three children were screaming at once, and Sheila was already in the yard by the time Bo got to the door. She yelled for him to call an ambulance. He could see Andrew lying on the ground and had some notion of Lars maniacally running around. He wanted to investigate further, to be sure himself of what had happened. He'd made it halfway across the yard before she saw him.

"Did you call?" she yelled toward him, then looked down at the boy's leg. Bo followed her eyes, and for the first time since he'd become a father, the swell of emotion was too much. The lower part of Andrew's leg lay at an odd angle with something more disturbing: skin stretched taut and pink over a sharp something. Bone. He thought he might vomit, but there was no time. He sprinted for the phone.

After calling, he grabbed a sofa pillow and some towels on his way back, unlocking the gate to the front yard.

"They're on the way; we're not to move him," he told Sheila in as calm a voice as he could muster, helping her to ease the pillow under Andrew's head, which was now in Sheila's lap.

The yard was completely fenced-in—a kind of stockade thing. Though not very attractive, it was considered a plus when they'd rented, and then purchased, the house. Childless at first, they liked the idea of privacy. Sheila had wanted a large garden. He fancied sleeping out with her under the stars. For a couple of years it was useful to these purposes, but now it had a swing and slide set as a centerpiece, a sand box, and a wildly unkempt look post-winter. The fence was in need of varnishing. Sheila still tried to garden in the summer, but her ambitions had shrunk to tomatoes and squash and some perennial beds that never quite lived up to expectations. The day would garner so many images for him in the future, but he would always remember, as they waited for the ambulance, wondering how many weekends it would take him to varnish the fence. All of this, in a matter of sixty seconds, went through Bo's mind.

In the ensuing twelve minutes of waiting, Bo and Sheila learned a lot of things. An unattended six-year-old could easily shimmy up a swing chain and walk across the crossbar. A child with a serious fracture could get very pale, and after bloodcurdling cries could become very quiet—worryingly quiet. And months of psychiatric therapy could be undone in a matter minutes. Parents can never, not ever, be prepared for some of what life has in store for them.

Sheila's gaze swung as she watched Lars making his rounds around them. She turned toward Genuine, who stood next to Andrew's bad side. The girl's eyes were bright, her face flushed.

"Gen, honey, take Lars and walk around the yard until the ambulance comes." Then she spoke more soothing words for Andrew, who was sweating and emitting occasional soft moans.

Bo didn't know what to do but wait. He knelt beside his wife and son, put a hand on his son's forehead.

Genuine took Lars over to the wet and weedy sand box, a large area bordered by railroad ties. She sat him down on the edge of a tie and seemed to have a little chat. Even from a distance, Bo could see the bright pink in his daughter's cheeks.

She came back to where they were on the grass with Andrew, Lars remaining behind. "I can fix him."

Bo was a little slow on the uptake. Minutes had passed since he'd called for the ambulance. He felt dazed by the introduction of another element. But Sheila was quick.

"Genevieve!" And then his wife lost all of her command. "Jesus Christ. Jesus fucking Christ!"

Bo's first response was, "Sheila!" But he put his arm around her. "Shhh, it's okay. It will be okay. They should be here soon. I told them to come straight to the backyard."

He glanced back toward the gate and again at Genuine, who now sat by Andrew's swollen leg. Her eyes shone like a fevered animal. Her hand reached toward the leg.

"Gen, honey, do not touch Andrew's leg. You'll hurt him." He tried for logic, for something to sway her attention.

Sheila looked up, and for that moment, Bo was glad that she was anchored to the ground by Andrew's head. He had no idea what she would do if she got to Genuine.

In the beginning of Genuine's troubles last year, Bo would come home to ask his wife, "How are things?" He would be invariably treated to the ways in which Genuine had tried, that day, to prove herself to her mother. Any day that one of the boys might have a fever or cold, or if Sheila had a headache, Genuine was there with her "healing hands." She would become frustrated and upset when she found they were not better.

Sheila had tried distraction and signed her up for ballet. Nothing changed. The child became obsessed. She brought it up every day. Sheila lost patience. The relationship between mother and daughter became contentious, each harboring her own suspicions. The weird flushing of Genuine's cheeks, and then her entire body, continued. Tests were done. They lived through fears of brain tumors, hormonal imbalances, and genetic anomalies. After all, the strange black hair. Even routine trips to the pediatrician were problematic. The child constantly reached out to sick children, alarming Sheila further with possibilities of contagion—not to mention the embarrassment she felt.

Bo became nervous on his daily drive home. The strain on his relationship with his wife was considerable. The child was intractable in her beliefs. If only they would believe her, she'd say, it would work again. Bo was willing to humor the child to prove her wrong. Sheila was reluctant, but they tried. Nothing changed. Genuine started doing poorly in school. Sister Dorothy inquired about what was going on at home.

Though they argued over Genuine daily, they were in agreement about keeping the nun out of the loop. At least they had convinced Genuine to keep a lid on it at school. Finally, the pediatrician had recommended Dr. Wittstein. Bo was the reluctant one then.

"I can't do this without professional help," Sheila had said. "It's been four months."

"She's only eight," was Bo's reply. He was a reserved man and couldn't imagine sharing his feelings in any kind of clinical setting. He knew that he'd most likely be required to.

"Do we let her go on with this until she's ten? Fifteen? How long?"

They were sitting in a familiar neighborhood restaurant. Nothing fancy, but an easy place to catch some privacy when they could wrangle a babysitter. They'd been coming here more and more. Their nights out had devolved to this. Just another place to carry on their one conversation. Bo had no more energy. Perhaps it would help.

"Okay," he said.

It did help, though not right away. Sessions with the three of them were not as hard as the initial sessions they had to have alone with the doctor. Over time, Dr. Wittstein spent more time alone with Genuine, with Sheila getting the update after waiting in his lobby. It seemed to be slow going, or not going at all. When Bo would ask if there were anything new, Sheila would just reply, "Next question."

But during this last month, things had gotten better. Genuine seemed happier and had, at Dr. Wittstein's suggestion, quit talking about healing to anyone, including her mother. Sheila took this as a good sign and started to relax. She got Genuine started on some crafts at home and taught her how to use the sewing machine. She seemed determined to get her focused on some other track, as if some activity could close a gate behind her, banishing her from fantasyland.

Sheila didn't talk to Bo much about Dr. Wittstein anymore. For several weeks now, she had refrained from talking about Genuine's "troubles" at all. They had sex more in the last month than they'd had in the previous six.

⟡—◇—⟡

Now he saw all of the past months' progress come undone—here, with his son's leg lying like a split tree branch, red and blue mounding around the bone, which remained barely under the skin. Again, he had the urge to vomit.

"Bo!" Sheila startled him. "Get her away from him."

"Please, Daddy," Genuine pleaded. Though he'd seen it before, he was unsettled by the high color in her cheeks.

Bo looked at his wife.

"Genuine, stay away." Sheila's tone was quiet and deadly.

Bo knew the only thing that could make matters worse would be for him to say yes to his daughter. He nodded to Genuine anyway, acknowledging to himself that his life had just changed in some fundamental way. He knew he'd uncorked a dark, sleeping storm in his wife, one that could cause lasting damage.

"Just his ankle, gently." It was too much, he thought, to fight the child in the midst of all this. He longed for peace in all things. He longed for the life he'd had thirty minutes before.

Genuine slid her hand from the grass and placed it on Andrew's ankle, inched it up slightly, stopping before the swelling. Bo heard Sheila suck in her breath and felt feel her look his way, but he kept his eyes on his daughter. Andrew's face was clammy and pale. Sheila had been stroking his arm, but he was still now, unmoving. Bo felt Sheila might be holding her breath, holding back all the things she wanted to let out. Holding back until she was ready to explode. He kept his eyes on Genuine.

Not much time passed, seconds at most, but it seemed to him a very long while. Years after, he would still remember that moment when everything stopped, when he didn't hear the birds, or Lars, or Andrew, or Genuine. And then everything was in motion, chaotic, noisy motion. Lars ran around in circles again. Ambulance sirens blared. Sheila was saying something—screaming? Genuine was on the ground, unconscious.

Later, when he belabored the moment in his memory, he would remember looking at Genuine in time to see her deeply flushed face go slack and her eyes roll back as she slumped to the ground. They'll need two stretchers, he'd thought. Lars replaced his earlier shouting with the similarly repetitive, "What happened to Gen? What happened to Gen?" As Bo's mind came back again to his daughter, he stood and carefully stepped around Andrew to get to her just as he heard the gate and the noise of incoming people and equipment. Sheila moved Andrew's head slightly, taking care, Bo could see, to cradle it back on the pillow.

"Bo," she said.

Bo had turned to greet the paramedics.

"Bo," Sheila said, louder.

He turned and saw that she was looking at Andrew's leg. Genuine's hand, which he hadn't noticed before, was still holding Andrew's leg below where the break was. But what? He didn't see the break. He looked at the other leg. No break. He looked at Sheila, but she was looking at Genuine, who seemed peaceful, as if she were asleep. A whole new paroxysm of sounds came from Sheila's mouth—guttural, primitive—as she knelt down beside her daughter. Stroking her hair, saying, first in a quiet voice, "Wake up, honey." Then louder. And louder.

By this time, the paramedics, though slightly confused, removed Sheila and focused on Genuine. Andrew was now standing, looking a little dazed. His legs appeared unremarkable. No bruising, no swelling. Both children were put on gurneys and loaded into the ambulance. There wasn't room for either parent. Bo, Sheila, and Lars were in the car and ready to go when the ambulance pulled away.

They didn't speak much on the way. One of them would start, look at the other, and then glance back at Lars, who was busy running a toy car up and down his seat belt. They each shook their head several times.

"You saw it, right?" Sheila asked.

Bo nodded, keeping his eyes on the road. He wanted to stay as close to the ambulance as possible.

"How could she . . . ?" Sheila again. And then, "Oh my God, all this time."

Genuine had, in fact, roused before the ambulance left. But because the paramedics had seen her unconscious, they started an IV and loaded her along with Andrew, who seemed perfectly fine to them. They had protocol to follow, as well as the word of the parents who witnessed the boy's fall. Genuine cried like any nine-year-old who gets an IV and is taken from her parents. Andrew seemed to take it all in stride.

Arriving at the hospital, Bo looked at Sheila before turning off the car. He knew her, how she'd be going over the past year, excoriating herself for all the ways she had wronged the child. He was contemplating the other direction, toward their unknowable future. A future unexpected, unplanned for, and probably, he thought, unwanted.

Alice Dunphy

October 5, 1987

It wasn't fair. That's all Alice could think, though she supposed she was getting her comeuppance for all those times she'd told the children that life wasn't meant to be fair. A stock response, she realized now with decades of hindsight. But this was different. This wasn't a toy unshared or the broken heart of a twelve-year-old; it was her life. Today was Alice Dunphy's seventieth birthday. She had now lived more years than anyone else in her family. All her grandparents had died before she was born, and her mother had passed away at the mere age of fifty. Alice's father, God bless him, lived until the ripe old age (for his time) of sixty-eight. John, Alice's husband, had not been so lucky, dying a year short of that mark.

Sitting with plastic tubing snaking its way up and around the back of her neck and over her head, Alice felt the cheat of this short-lived longevity. Her life had been full, true, but she wasn't done—didn't feel done. And the indignity of sitting here, frail and failing in the rectory of this church, here, where she had spent much of her adult life energetically catering to its needs in all manners of activity, here, on her birthday, most assuredly her last, was too much to bear. In addition, she was being fawned over by that ridiculous Father Hanson. It was too much, all too very much.

"Mrs. Dunphy, I'm so glad you could come today," the priest said as soon as her eldest son Jack had arranged her wheelchair and tank. Her children were taking turns fussing over her in her dyingness. Three of the five lived in the area, and she'd had to put up with their constant phone calls and ministrations. Nilda, her home health aide, could have very well driven her here, but since it was her birthday, Jack insisted. Or perhaps Linda, his wife, had insisted.

When they'd first pulled up to the rectory, Alice was happy to see the yellow and purple chrysanthemums in full bloom along the front border. The trees, according to their types, were either shedding or holding on to their leaves until colder weather came to bite them off. Fall had long been her favorite season—though she suspected her preference had begun when she'd finally had all five children in school. She remembered the sharp smell of dried leaves riding in on dry, Indian summer winds and the cool nights that begat crisp mornings. She used to stand in her backyard after the children went off to school and mark the slow parade of color as the trees and plants faded toward winter. It had been some time since she'd stood like that in her yard.

When Jack opened the door to help her out of the car, he'd asked, yet again, if she wouldn't like him to stay for lunch. Alice quickly forgot about the colors. He'd stood, with the wheelchair by his side, reaching for her hand. She could walk well enough to the rectory, but he wouldn't have it. The oxygen tank was to keep her from getting out of breath. Jack was also her cardiologist. Her strength was diminished and would only get worse. He knew—she knew—how sick she was. She didn't like the reminders.

"Jack Dunphy, thank you for picking me up and taking me here, but please go play golf. It's your day off."

"It's your birthday, Mother."

Alice's exasperation was about to get the better of her, she felt, so she patted Jack on the arm and said, "I know, Jack. We'll have fun with everyone this weekend. Nilda will pick me up here at two-thirty."

She got into the wheelchair and said, "I'm fine." And again, as he pushed her toward the door, "I'm fine."

Just before Jack left, she'd insisted on sitting in a real chair. "Okay, Mother, but I insist that you use the oxygen."

Alice had a sincere desire to swat her son as he guided her by the elbow from her wheelchair to a parlor chair. He kissed her on the head, as if she were a child, said, "Happy birthday, Mother," and left.

Her children were planning a party for the weekend at her daughter Margaret's large house by the museum. Margaret's husband was an attorney. All five of Alice's children and thirteen grandchildren would be there for what Alice considered her send-off party, though they'd offered other plausible excuses: Columbus Day weekend coinciding with her landmark seventieth, and some "just happened" to be flying through Des Moines on their way to somewhere else. Their efforts were exhausting her. And now, Father Hanson, babbling on.

"The school children have arranged a lovely little bit of entertainment for you," the priest told her, "and then we'll have lunch."

Alice remembered her mother had often used the word "lovely." It seemed to go in and out of fashion. She didn't know why it irritated her that Father Hanson should use it. But then again, everything he did irritated her. She wouldn't have come here today if it weren't for Patrick O'Halloran's insistence.

"Where's Monsignor O'Halloran?" she asked.

Alice Dunphy had been good friends with Monsignor Patrick O'Halloran for nearly a lifetime. Two years her senior, he had been a childhood friend of her brother Thomas and her husband John. The young Patrick O'Halloran had also been her first kiss.

The Dunphys were already living in this suburb of Des Moines when Patrick was transferred from a parish in Minnesota to St. Timothy's. She and John had campaigned for his transfer when the position became available, and Patrick had been grateful to be close to what he considered his only remaining family. He was Margaret's godfather and had christened each of their children, even when the Dunphys needed to make a trip to Minnesota for the occasion.

"He called to say that we should enjoy the children without him, and he'll join us for lunch," Father Hanson said.

Alice raised an eyebrow to the priest. The phrasing didn't sound particularly like Patrick, and he would know that she would be perturbed by his absence.

Father Hanson regrouped. "Apparently there was a last-minute something the bishop needed him for." Patrick, at seventy-two, was still going strong.

Patrick, now long a monsignor, had left St. Timothy's some years before to work in the bishop's office downtown. It wasn't far, and Alice often went to hear Patrick say Mass. At least she used to.

"How long have you known Monsignor O'Halloran?"

She looked at the priest and felt all of her little annoyances bubbling up. He'd made a poor initial impression when he first arrived in Iowa, casting about like a prince wrongfully sent to Siberia. Alice was not one to forgive quickly, nor forget. She knew she should give him the benefit of the doubt for his efforts on her behalf today, and she felt the slightest momentary twinge of guilt for not meeting him in the middle. In the middle of what? In the middle of her dislike for him? For this dislike that had brought a subtle remonstrance from Patrick? Though she was sure Patrick disliked him, too. Father Hanson was an obviously ambitious man and could barely hide an air of subtle condescension. Not everyone caught it. Patrick said that she was mistaken, but he had been unconvincing.

Since Patrick had left St. Timothy's, there had been three priests assigned to the parish, so she couldn't say that she resented Father Hanson for taking Patrick's place. The first priest to come was an older—though not as old as Alice was now—local man, Father McKee, who had spent several years teaching at a school in Nebraska and retired from St. Timothy's after two years. The next one, Father Riley, had been young and popular with the women. It didn't turn out well. Then came Father Hanson, somehow transferred from the Philadelphia diocese.

"Were you childhood friends?" Father Hanson had positioned his chair too close to hers. It was not in its usual place; she knew this room well. Some of the other furniture had been re-arranged, she supposed, for the children's performance, whatever that might entail. Undoubtedly there would be some spilling into the main hallway. There were impressions in the large Aubusson, squared off in symmetry where chairs and tables had been moved. She had seen this rug before on previous visits. Father Hanson had brought it with him when he was transferred.

"Yes, we were," she answered, hoping he would quit asking questions. She eyed the expensive rug. The floral motif struck her as somehow inappropriate for a priest's dwelling, though she hadn't detected any other leanings in him, and she had a sharp eye for that kind of thing. After all, there was her son Tommy.

"The rug was my mother's," Hanson said. He was too observant, Alice thought, too cunning. He must know that she had furnished this parlor herself, so many years ago when Patrick had first come to be the pastor. The furniture had been a gift from her and John to welcome their friend. The chair she sat in, the striped wing-back, used to grace John's office. She'd passed it along after he died.

"Will the children arrive soon?" Let's get on with it, she thought.

"Yes, they should be here anytime. More tea?"

It seemed to her that Father Hanson's behavior today was just to the right of obsequious, as if there were something he were angling for. He knew she'd already made her will and was leaving some money for the school. But there wouldn't be more—she had a large family, after all.

But in fairness, her illness begat the attention. The problem with looking frail, being frail, she thought, was that you couldn't forget about your illness. People just took too much notice.

This Father Hanson was forty-two, she remembered. She'd read it somewhere, perhaps in the résumé that Patrick had shown her. You'll be here, too, she thought. Twenty-eight years is a very short time. Click your heels and you'll be here, having everyone being so solicitous and pitying, thinking they'll never get to this spot, like somehow they'll be spared.

Fifty-two years is a short time, too. Fifty-two years ago, Patrick O'Halloran had followed her into the kitchen during her brother Thomas's birthday celebration, tilted her chin up, and kissed her. He was to leave for seminary in the fall, so it took her by surprise. She'd been trying to get John Dunphy's attention all summer, but she gave herself over to the sweetness of it anyway.

Her mother had walked in on them. "Mary Alice Kelly!" They had both slunk back into the dining room, pink and disturbed enough for John and Thomas to notice. Later, Patrick had said, "I shouldn't have done that," and then, "You shouldn't have let me."

John, Patrick, and Thomas were the only kind of friends that boys knew how to be—competitive—which worked in Alice's favor. She'd told Thomas about the kiss, and he'd told John, who couldn't stand the fact that he might have overlooked something, that Alice might be worth pursuing. John took a new interest in her, and Patrick's conscience never plagued him after that. It was 1933, and though it was the depth of the depression, they'd managed to come through. Alice remembered those years as some of the sweetest in her life.

The three boys had been her idols, adventurous and funny. She had lived vicariously through their antics growing up in St. Paul. The boys were also smart, and they competed at school. John managed to get himself into the University of Minnesota, married to Alice, and then into medical school. Patrick got himself into seminary. Thomas joined the police force like their father. Then they all went off to the war, and the sweetness was gone. Thomas was killed during the landing of Normandy. Thomas, she thought now, oh Thomas.

The loss of Thomas had cemented the friendship between Patrick and John, and for the most part, Alice was happy to be in the middle of it. They'd had happy years, but John's death five years before had been as big a blow to Patrick as it had been to her—bigger, perhaps. The men had shared things that they didn't share with Alice: the war, the romantic view of their boyhood days, and perhaps other things Alice didn't know about. She knew John's view of life, though deeply Catholic, precluded grave theological concerns. Patrick had a deeper conscience, deeper struggles. John was a surgeon, interested in cutting things out. That wasn't to say he wasn't a good doctor. He was, but Alice knew that surgery had been a good choice for him.

"Mrs. Dunphy?" Father Hanson was standing perched by her teacup, pot in hand, ready to pour. There was a small folding table in front of her. It seemed a little unstable. She looked around now, wondering where the antique tea table had gone, the one she had bought so many years ago. Perhaps taken away to make room for the children.

On days when Alice was feeling particularly weak, Nilda would give her tea on the metal tray attached to her wheelchair so that she could watch the birds out her back window.

Nilda had found the tray at a medical supply store and made a bag for it. She looked over at the empty wheelchair and thought perhaps she should have stayed in it.

Nilda was a good aide, always cheerful and compliant. Though Jack would give her instructions on how much his mother should be allowed to do, and what she could do, Nilda always let Alice set the tone for the day. Alice had a few bridge friends who would come on Tuesdays, and if she wasn't feeling up to playing, they would just sit and have some tea and sandwiches. Nilda always put out a good spread.

Nilda could ruin a day for Alice, too, if she talked too much. Her imperfect grammar could set Alice's brain on fire. Alice knew she was quick to overreact, which she thought had more to do with her heart than her brain. After all, she had heart failure, and it was failing her in more ways than one. Her devotion to Christ, Mary, and all of the saints (particularly St. Timothy, whom she'd adopted as a kind of patron saint) seemed to have shrunk down to a black nut in her chest—like the black walnuts lying around in her yard these days, the grandchildren no longer interested in gathering them, let alone her busy children. Oh, she remembered, Jack had the tree cut down last year.

She prayed and read books about saints, but she wouldn't talk to Patrick about what was in her heart. Though interested in the most delicate points of theology, Patrick always felt that faith itself was the answer. Faith could be blind, unreasonable, and uncaring, but it was the only way to realize an approach to God. She knew what Patrick would say.

Alice needed relief from her fear of dying and something to soothe the blackness. She also knew that it wasn't her illness and impending death that had broken her faith. It was only now that she could admit it to herself. There had been tiny cracks over the years, cracks she had glazed over.

The first one had been the death of Thomas during the war. It had been a great and inconsolable loss to Alice. She had two younger brothers, but Thomas had been her champion, her confidant, her comfort. He'd been the best man at her wedding and godfather to Jack. She'd gotten over it in time, in her own way, but it was the first time she'd resented God.

Alice looked at Father Hanson, still standing with the teapot ready, and put her hand over her cup.

"No, no thank you, Father," she said.

"I'll just go check with Mrs. Stoltz about the lunch." He nodded and left her.

Well, she thought, he knew when to back away. She wished Patrick had been here on time.

As their lives progressed and the children grew up, Alice often felt at odds with her men, as she thought of them. Patrick and John played golf, attended football games, and held long discussions out of earshot in John's little den. John served on some diocesan boards, thanks to Patrick, though more for his stature as a doctor than for any other reason. John's life centered on routine: work time, mealtime, leisure time. He had a sharp intelligence, but Alice often thought he lacked a basic curiosity about things. John enjoyed the children when they were behaving and ignored them when they weren't. He wasn't interested in the why of their behavior. He had ignored Tommy for ten years. There had been no time for deathbed reconciliation.

Patrick would engage in discussion with her, but it always led to the same thing: basic trust in faith. Alice often felt that Patrick deemed her unworthy of deeper theological discussion. Perhaps she was, but she couldn't reconcile the church's view about Tommy. She'd been quick to condemn Tommy in the beginning, thinking that if he'd only had faith he could overcome his tendencies, but over time, she came to realize he was made the way he was. She couldn't just let her youngest go, nor could she constantly battle with him about his life. So she accepted it, though she had to admit that she didn't like to think about it too carefully. Surprisingly, Patrick had supported her.

"You're his mother," Patrick had said. "Your only job is to love him."

That was more than John could do, though she hadn't believed it was about faith or what the church said. His shame was more personal, more self-centered. But once she let go, once she accepted who Tommy was, all the little things she had been stifling started to percolate and steam.

In retrospect, she knew it had been necessary to keep everything in her life humming along lest she notice things too closely: the petty bickering in choir, the meanness she detected in some of the nuns who taught her children, and the rumors she'd heard but ignored about Father McKee. And her friends, all Catholic, always polite when Tommy's name came up, but eager, she knew, to move past him to her other children or to change the subject.

At least Tommy was coming this weekend, too. That was a plus. He would make her laugh.

Alice was still alone when she heard a commotion in the hall-way and felt relief that the events were finally going to move the day along. She could hear the principal, Sister Dorothy, greeting the housekeeper.

"Good morning, Helen."

Everyone in the parish knew Helen Stoltz, who had worked in the rectory for thirty years. Father Hanson, to his credit, still addressed her more formally as "Mrs. Stoltz."

Father Hanson reappeared with Sister Dorothy, a tall, beak-nosed woman who rarely let the children see her smile—or adults, for that matter—though Alice knew the nun to be a very competent administrator. Most of the nuns who had taught her children were long gone, except for old Sister Benedict, who no longer taught but took care of the convent, or at least was allowed to think that was her job. Vocations had been down for years, and the school had more lay teachers now than nuns. The nuns no longer wore habits, of course, but could be recognized by their plain garb and the medals pinned on their chests, or the long ribbon and cross that Sister Dorothy wore.

Until recently, Alice had remained very involved in the life of the school and knew most of the teachers by sight. It was Carol Miller, the fifth-grade teacher, who accompanied Sister Dorothy and the children now. It appeared to be a mixed group of grades, perhaps fourth through eighth—Alice had a hard time these days guessing children's ages. Some of the girls looked like eighteen-year-olds. She was surprised that all of the fifteen or so students fit comfortably in the rearranged parlor—three rows of five. It was an unusual occasion to have a select group of children perform, leading Alice to believe the children were likely picked by lottery. It spared the teachers accusations of favoritism by the parents. It hadn't been that way when her children were in school, but parents were getting more involved these days.

The children first performed a long poem about Columbus and

then a couple of her favorite hymns. She knew Patrick was responsible, through Father Hanson or Sister Dorothy, for their choices. They even did a reasonable job with "Panis Angelicus," considering the range of ages, thanks particularly to a very tall girl with an impressive high soprano voice. At the end, each student came forward and presented various gifts: some flowers, a box of candy, and cards from each of the classes. Sister Dorothy did her usual prodding and restraining, keeping order and control. The younger children came forward timidly; the few older boys seemed bored.

There was one black-haired child whom Alice knew she'd never seen before. Her heavy eyebrows rode her forehead like small caterpillars, but she was otherwise pretty. The child was clutching a card but hanging back, Alice could see. Ah well, she thought, I'd be scared to come up to me, too. She appeared to be about ten. The thought of her youth undid Alice for a moment. She wished to have life rolling out in front of her instead of behind.

As the children gave their gifts, Miss Miller led them past a large platter of cookies Alice had sent ahead from the bakery, then out of the parlor to line up, two by two, at the door. Sister Dorothy stood sentinel, making sure each child took only one, though there were ten dozen. When Alice protested, Sister Dorothy said, "They shouldn't spoil their appetites before lunch."

"Then please take them to share with the rest of their classmates." Alice had been strict this way with her own children in her time. She couldn't see the point in it anymore. Life was so short.

Father Hanson excused himself to find Mrs. Stoltz to wrap up the cookies. The dark-haired child moved away from the others and backed into the corner of the room.

"Genevieve, bring your card to Mrs. Dunphy." Sister Dorothy never missed a trick. The child shuffled forward and took her place behind the last few children and their offerings. She kept her attention on Alice, looking from her face to the oxygen tank and back. There seemed to be something about the child that kept Sister Dorothy's attention, made her nervous. She must be slipping, Alice thought. Sister Dorothy rarely let anything derail her.

Finally, Genevieve was the last one left.

"Come here, child," Alice said. "You can't catch what I have."

"What's in the tank?" she asked.

"Genevieve!" Sister Dorothy said.

However, Alice was amused by the circumstances and shot Sister Dorothy a warning look. At least the child had nerve. Tommy had been like this, inquisitive and sometimes lacking boundaries.

"It's oxygen," she said. "My lungs don't work as well as they should."

"Does it hurt?"

"I get short of breath, and then it's hard for me to do things."

The girl cocked her head. "Are you going to die?"

Sister Dorothy had her hand on the girl's shoulder in a flash, fingers curling into the flesh as she pulled the child away.

"Time to go, Genevieve. Go out and get in line with the other children."

"No, let her stay," Alice said, although if someone had asked her why, she wouldn't have been able to answer.

The child had not yet presented her card to Alice and now held it out, though still restrained at the shoulder by the nun. Alice looked up at Sister Dorothy again. The nun withdrew her hand.

"Yes, Genevieve. That's your name? Yes, I am going to die."

"Are you scared?" she asked.

Sister Dorothy gasped. "I'm sorry, Mrs. Dunphy. I really must take the children back to school now."

Alice waved her hand in impatience. She was beginning to have fun. At least this was interesting. "Why, yes, I am," she said. She could hear a muffled squawk at the back of Sister Dorothy's throat. Now they were both in trouble, she thought. This Genevieve's forthrightness was catching.

The child held out the card, and Alice reached for it. It was a card from the second-grade children, a store-bought birthday card with children's names printed every which way all over both sides.

While she was reading the card, the child took a step closer to Alice's chair and put her hand on Alice's arm, surreptitiously, out of the nun's sightline.

She took the child's hand and said, "I'm so happy to have met you, Genevieve." With her other hand, Alice reached for one of the girl's long braids. "My daughters used to wear their hair like this. It's very pretty."

The hand she was holding was warm, nearly hot. She released the braid and looked up. The child's face was flushed now. She looked gravely at Alice and said, "I don't think . . ." and then went white and fell toward the floor.

Father Hanson came back into the room the same moment Alice rushed out of her seat to catch the child. The tray and teacup went flying while Alice sank to the floor with Genevieve, knocking over the oxygen tank on the way down. Though Sister Dorothy was quick to come to her aid, Alice had time to think about the weight of the girl's head as she released a braid that was trapped under the tank. Father Hanson helped Alice up as the nun carried the girl to the sofa. She was removing the oxygen tubing from her face when Patrick O'Halloran walked in. Imposing, she thought, in his full monsignor attire—black cassock with its purple cincture, shining gray hair peeking out under his biretta. She knew he did this for Father Hanson as much as for the occasion of her birthday. He took a quick glance around the room and asked, "Has anyone called an ambulance?"

Patrick was quick to Alice's side. "Here, let's get the oxygen back on," he said, reaching down to right the canister.

Alice, though relieved to have him here, waved him off. "No, leave it for now." Then to the room in general, "Call an ambulance!" But the child was waking up, and Father Hanson, glancing around the room, said, "I'll go call her mother."

Genevieve's color was coming back, and Sister Dorothy, to her credit, sat next to her on the sofa and held her hand. "She just fainted;

she'll be fine." That took away the credit. The girl looked around the room and settled her eyes on Alice, who stood and made her way to the couch.

"How do you feel?" Alice asked.

"A little dizzy." The girl shifted her eyes to the oxygen tubing lying on the floor.

"Sister Dorothy, perhaps Genevieve could have some water."

The nun nodded and left. Alice took her place on the sofa. Now it was just Patrick, Alice, and the girl.

Patrick asked, "What happened?"

Before Alice could speak, the child answered, "I don't know."

"You fainted, dear. I think you should lie down here until your mother comes," Alice said.

"I'm okay. How are you?"

Of all her children and grandchildren, including Tommy, Alice had never known any of them to be as self-possessed as this child. Perhaps her granddaughter Liza, who was fourteen, but not at this age.

"How old are you, Genevieve?" she asked.

"Ten."

"What's your last name?"

"Eriksson."

"I don't think I know your family. Did you move here recently?"

"No, we've always lived here, but we're not Catholics," she said, just as Sister Dorothy was returning with a glass of water.

Patrick had gotten Alice's wheelchair and installed the oxygen tank on its platform. He wheeled the chair to the sofa and proffered her oxygen tubing again. His biretta, with its purple pom-pom, now sat on the coffee table.

"I'll be fine without the tank for a bit."

"You don't need it anymore," the child said.

Alice heard the avowal in the child's voice but read it as a question. Sister Dorothy made her sucking sound again, as she turned to

Patrick and said, "Genevieve seems fine. Monsignor, I think it might be better to bring her back to the school to wait for her mother. She can lie down in the nurse's office." She took the child's water glass and set it on the coffee table. She looked toward the hallway and the noisy school children in queue.

"No, no, Sister. Her mother is already on her way." Father Hanson had returned to the parlor. "If you could please wait, too, Sister, but let the others go back to school."

The child was becoming less flushed, and Alice doubted that ten minutes had elapsed. The child did seem to be fine. Perhaps she hadn't had breakfast. You can never tell these days with parents. Perhaps her mother worked outside the home.

Alice took the child's hand again. It was cool to the touch, and she remembered how hot it had been before. The child squeezed back and gave her a look that Alice could only judge to be reassuring, though she couldn't imagine what for.

Returned from her duty at the door, Sister Dorothy stood at the edge of the parlor, taking it all in. Between the child and the nun, Alice felt overly scrutinized. She turned to Father Hanson and said, "I'd like to use your restroom."

Both Patrick and Father Hanson jumped up and offered to accompany her, but she waved them away.

"I've been here countless times. I can manage on my own, thank you."

She was nearly to the end of the hallway when she realized she hadn't brought her purse. She wanted to check her makeup and be sure that something wasn't amiss. On her way back to the parlor, she heard some hushed voices.

"Two or three months at the most." Oh Lord. She knew it was true, but it was more true coming from Patrick's mouth. She shouldn't be surprised that he'd talked to Jack, but, well, she didn't like to hear it, not from his mouth to Father Hanson's ears. In front of the child, too. People could be so thoughtless.

"I don't think she's going to die," Genevieve said. "Not for a long time, anyway."

Alice was standing as close to the door as she could without being seen. She felt like a child. She liked this Genevieve more and more and wondered what her parents were like.

"Genevieve, that's enough," Sister Dorothy said in her most pre-emptive tone, like a parent who chides a child for a recurring behavior, as if this discussion had been had before.

"It's all right, Sister," Patrick said, "it was a scary thing for me to say. I'm sorry, Genevieve. No one really knows when God will call somebody home to Him. Perhaps Mrs. Dunphy will get better."

"She already is," the child said.

"Well, you've had quite the morning, Genevieve, and I'm sure Mrs. Dunphy would be happy that you are thinking well of her," Patrick said.

Alice made some noise and rounded the corner into the parlor.

"I just need to get my handbag," she said. "Genevieve, I'm so happy you are thinking well of me." She shot Patrick a look and avoided the others, slipping back out of the room. That would shut them up.

She felt exhilarated. She hadn't felt this well in months. It must be the adrenaline of the day. Or perhaps she was closer to death than even they thought, having her one last hurrah, as she'd heard some dying people do. Suddenly, she was very hungry.

Tread Carefully

April 1988

"She was sick," Genuine said.

"Yes, we know, honey, but you can't heal just anyone. We've talked about this," Bo said, striving to keep exasperation out of his voice. The evening was wearing on, the boys already asleep. The conversation went round and round with little sign of progress or cooperation from his daughter. She's only eleven, he thought, how will we get through her teens?

The child shrugged and turned toward her mother, as if looking for a dissenting opinion.

"I think it's time for bed," Sheila said, raising an eyebrow as Genuine started to protest.

Bo reached for his daughter, kissed her on the forehead, and said, "Promise, remember? It's important."

She pulled away and looked from one parent to the other. "I want to get baptized."

Both parents let out deep sighs.

"Not tonight, Gen," Sheila said. "No more talk tonight."

"I still want to," she declared from the top of the stairs.

They sat quietly, waiting to hear the sounds of the bathroom and then the bedroom die off, knowing that a reprisal might be forthcoming.

Bo wanted the details of this newest idea, the religious conversion, or whatever it was to be called. Sheila only said, "Later," and stood. He followed her up the stairs.

They'd had a nighttime routine, one of their own, not involving the children—well, only passively involving them. It started when the children were very young and began to sleep through the night. They would tiptoe into their rooms and gaze at their sleeping off-spring. In the beginning, there was a feeling of wonder. One, for the fact that they were asleep. Two, for the sheer beauty of them in their slumbering unawareness.

Years went by, but the routine stayed the same. Even if they'd been out late and caught in an urgent hum toward their own bed, they would stop and gaze in wonder that one could sleep with merely half a body in the bed while another slept bound up in a tight cocoon of tangled and sweaty bed linens. They were sometimes astonished that they'd survived another day as parents, that the children continued to grow out of bounds of their expectations, and that all of the noise and chaos and moodiness would settle each night into this unearthly quiet. This was their daily reward, this hammer that had stopped hitting, this silence.

They looked in on the boys first: Lars the cliffhanger, Andrew the chrysalis. Genuine was asleep, too, thankfully, her hair a halo of blackness feathered out on the pillow like a peacock's tail. The child was proud of her hair and resisted her mother's motions to cut it to a more manageable length. As she pulled the door shut, Sheila said, "Perhaps we should let her."

"Catholic?" Bo said. "Absolutely not."

Sheila was too bound up in her own emotions to bring the discussion to the bedroom, but she couldn't sleep. She resented Bo for once more putting her outside whatever discussion he was having with himself, if he was having one. If he wasn't, then she resented him more—especially for the way he could fall asleep and leave her stranded and alone in her wakefulness.

During the months after the event of Andrew's leg, Sheila and Bo had come together in a communion of parenthood vastly different from the fretful year leading up to it. They were, after all, the only parents they knew in the entire world whose child had exhibited such ability. This was something quite different from realizing your child might actually become that Olympian or Nobel scientist you'd been secretly wishing for. For whatever reason their daughter was singled out, the fact that she was theirs and only theirs (and her brothers, too, of course) brought the parents closer than they had ever been. They could talk to no one else. Telling Sheila's mother was out of the question. The woman understood the meaning of a secret as something to be told carefully to many people, one at a time. Telling Bo's parents would also have its own challenges. Though Genuine was their oldest grandchild, they had formed more natural bonds with her brothers and still viewed her looks as something outside the possibility of their gene pool.

Sheila and Bo intuitively knew that secrecy was best. Their pride was not so great that they didn't foresee the dangers of some modern freak show surrounding their child. They talked about it incessantly until they became if not comfortable, perhaps more at ease, with who they were and what their life might look like—at least for the years that Genuine was under their control.

They forbade the child from healing anyone outside the family, and never without one of them in attendance. Though Bo and Sheila were interested to see how this ability might play out, they were also wary of how it might affect Genuine herself.

In any event, after Andrew's leg, Genuine's ability seemed to go dormant. It had no effect on a case of poison ivy that Lars contracted shortly after the first healing. Try as she might, Genuine couldn't "fix" her mother's migraine, a bruise Andrew had procured while skateboarding, nor any other small maladies that came her way for testing over the summer. She was impatient. Sheila found her in the yard one day trying to fix a worm that had been severed in two. That the child might have done this to the worm as part of her experimenting disturbed Sheila quite a bit, but Genuine insisted that she'd found the worm already bisected.

Curiously, the weird flushing had also disappeared—until it came back in late August when Bo came home from work with a nasty summer cold. He'd gone to work in the morning hopeful of feeling better with some over-the-counter meds, but by noon, he'd packed it in and drove home. Genuine, ever at the ready to lay her hands on something, made short work of it.

"It was a pulsing," Bo said. "I could feel it in her hands. They were warm, really warm, and I could feel the heat spreading." He was a little wide-eyed and dazed.

Genuine had not fainted, nor seemed fazed or surprised that the redness of her father's eyes and nose all seemed to go away in a matter of minutes. She smiled and tilted her head just so. The smugness disturbed Sheila, but not as much as the worm. They were in for a lot of unknowns, and she cautioned herself to go with the flow.

Andrew got the chickenpox first.

"I can make him better," Genuine said. Andrew had arrived home after an overnight trip with the Johnsons down the street. Apparently he'd been itching the whole time but didn't want to be taken home. Blisters seemed to be everywhere already: his torso, deep in his scalp, and beginning to bud on the palms of his hands. Sheila and Bo were still not convinced that their child might not experience some deleterious effect. This was more than a cold. But the combination of their son's misery and Genuine's relentless pursuit of what she considered her right to perform moved the parents to acquiesce.

Andrew was pox-free in close to half an hour. Genuine did not pass out this time either. Until the pox started to subside, she inspected Andrew's body and fretted in a way that reminded them of the previous year when she'd been doubted. Sheila knew it brought up feelings in all of them, feelings that were still too close for inspection.

A few days later, Lars broke out, but nothing Genuine did would help. He continued to spot increasingly each day for several days and gave Genuine a whopping case, too. Apparently she couldn't heal herself either. There were other small successes and failures, no fainting, and the child seemed happy enough to perform for her family. Secrecy was agreed upon—a risky agreement with children. Sheila and Bo worked together to keep everything else as normal as possible.

And now this. Even after what happened with Alice Dunphy (though they had been fairly sure the significance was known only to them), this morning Genuine had tried to "fix" her friend Julia Whitman. Julia and Genuine had been friends since the Whitmans moved to the neighborhood when the girls were three. Anne, Julia's mother, and Sheila were friends, but Anne had gone back to work after having Julia while Sheila stayed home with the boys as they came. When it didn't work out for Genuine at the public school, Sheila felt that Anne was a little miffed with her for taking Genuine away from Julia.

A bigger problem was their husbands, who were miles apart in compatibility. Dean Whitman was too talkative and overbearing for Bo's taste. Bo wasn't very interested in football, and Dean was a rabid Hawkeyes fan. It was hard, given the men, to keep up with dinner dates and other common occasions, though they were always included in whatever backyard barbecue the Whitmans had going on through the summer. Dean liked having lots of families and kids around, something that endeared him to Sheila. She'd felt privately, at times, that Bo was a little hard on Dean, but they were a bit older than the Erikssons—perhaps that counted for some of the difference. The women drifted somewhat, but the girls kept up. They spent many afternoons together in the early days of elementary school and still saw each other regularly. It had been very much less when Genuine was going through her "trial," as her parents now called it.

◇

Anne had called Sheila after the fact.

"Can you come over? I need to tell you something."

"Is Gen okay?" Sheila asked. It was a Saturday morning. The girls had arranged this playdate earlier in the week.

"Yes, she's fine. Can you come now?"

Sheila glanced around the kitchen—morning dishes half-done and the boys out back with Bo, who was raking leaves. Andrew and Lars seemed intent on re-directing his efforts.

"I've got to run over to the Whitmans'," she called out the back door to Bo, shutting the door before he had time to respond.

The Whitmans lived exactly fives houses away, but across the street and past the corner. When the girls were younger, Sheila would accompany Genuine and return to pick her up. In the early years, Julia would spend two afternoons a week with the Erikssons while her mother worked. Sheila wished now that she and Anne had not drifted. It would be easier to share information with someone she was close to. She was, in fact, very close to Kate Dixon, who also lived in the neighborhood and whose son Elliot was a friend to Lars. But she had not confided in Kate either.

Kate had a quick and satirical sense of humor that Sheila greatly admired. She was also not from the area; she was from Ohio, and while that wasn't really the East Coast, it was not really the Midwest either, no matter what the weatherman said. Then she realized, not for the first time, what her relationship lacked with Anne was an easy affability. Anne was serious, organized, and critical. Spending time with her could occasionally put Sheila in a dark place. But Sheila loved Julia, who was an easygoing kid like her dad and a good counter to Genuine's more intense character.

Anne opened the front door before Sheila reached the path from the sidewalk, and Sheila realized she hadn't seen Anne since August.

How can that much time slip by unnoticed? Anne needed a trip to the hairdresser, she thought. She was usually more meticulous, though it was Saturday and Sheila realized she herself had only briefly brushed her own hair many hours earlier, and she was entirely sure now that she hadn't put on any makeup.

"Did you know that Julia has the chickenpox?" Anne asked as she held the door open for Sheila.

"Oh, no, I'm sorry. Did she catch it from Genuine?" Perhaps she hadn't needed to worry about the other thing.

"Well, it doesn't matter. Julia's school is rife with it, too."

"You should have told me. I wouldn't have sent Gen over this morning, though she's had them, so there's no danger that way."

"Well, I did call and tell her not to come." Anne looked down the hall toward the bedrooms. This was a three-bedroom house with the same the beige brick as Sheila and Bo's, but it was a one-story ranch. The only thing that saved the neighborhood from complete homogeneity was the different style of homes and the varied size of the lots. The Whitmans' home stood further back from the street than the Erikssons', but had a much smaller backyard.

Sheila could guess what was coming. She followed Anne down the hall toward Julia's room.

The girls were busy on the floor with some type of board game. Only Julia looked up when the mothers stepped across the threshold. She didn't look at all poxy. Sheila's chest tightened as she watched Genuine continue to ignore her presence.

Julia stood up and came over to Sheila.

"Look, Mrs. Eriksson! Genuine cured my chickenpox!"

"She woke up covered in them this morning," Anne said.

"I don't . . ." Sheila replied as she thought, I don't know what I'm supposed to say. She wished Bo were here; he'd be thinking quicker than her. She looked down and said, "Gen, I think we should go home now."

Genuine finally looked over her shoulder at her mother, who could see that the child might be thinking of objecting. Instead, Genuine stood and mumbled, "Okay," as she looked at the floor.

"I would have called you right away, but she woke up so quickly and then begged me not to," Anne said.

"What?"

"She fainted. I'm sorry I haven't told you anything yet." Anne rushed on about how Genuine had shown up at their door and explained that she could visit anyway since she's already had the chickenpox. "I figured you knew."

Sheila was still catching up to what she knew and what she was supposed to know, all the while composing some sort of fiction that might make sense—something, anything, a stalling thing at least. She settled on redirection.

"You fainted?" She stroked the child's hair as any concerned mother might, though her concerns had not yet turned toward Genuine's welfare.

"Only for a minute, and I feel fine."

Sheila turned toward Anne. "Honestly, I don't know what to say. I think I should take her home and make sure she's not sick."

"I'm not sick, Mama. You know that."

"I don't know that at all, honey." She tried to sound soft and motherly.

"But what about the chickenpox?" Anne asked. She had a look that Sheila recognized; it reminded her of a terrier. Anne had never reminded her of a terrier before.

She turned to Julia and said, "I'm really glad you feel better." Then to Anne, "Thanks so much for calling. I'm sure she'll be fine," as she shouldered Genuine toward the door.

$$\diamond\!\!-\!\!\diamond\!\!-\!\!\diamond$$

It was true, they had agreed not to raise their children with the restriction of one religion, but they hadn't known what kind of children they were going to have when they'd decided all those years ago. Sheila had begun to suspect that Bo had a particular distaste for Catholics. She thought his feelings might be remnants of his upbringing, which she considered to be unfair prejudice for something he'd never really investigated.

Not that she wanted to run out and rejoin the Church either, but given Genuine's gift, she wasn't unwilling to investigate some greater meaning. The Catholics had some experience with this. She was fairly sure that it was well outside the purview of Lutheranism. Since Genuine herself was expressing interest, she wished that Bo would at least have the conversation. And another thing, she'd had another call from Mrs. Dunphy she hadn't told Bo about.

"Perhaps it's time we sent the kids to public school," Bo said. Sheila thought he'd been asleep.

"Alice Dunphy called today," she countered.

Cancer

April 1996

Kevin stood at the door to the rectory and hesitated, looking at the bell. He was having second thoughts, third thoughts—too many thoughts. Cancer. Testicles. Surgery. And his girlfriend, Cynthia.

Cynthia was a litigator in a small but prominent Philadelphia firm. Persuasion was not so much a technique for her as it was a way of life. It spilled over into their lives. It was what landed him here. In Iowa. At a church to see a so-called healer. He looked around at his surroundings, trying to shake the surreal unfamiliarity of his current situation: gray portentous sky flattening the light over a cluster of squat, beige brick buildings. A newer, larger building stood across the street, a high school with small young trees inside circles of protective wire. Even the early tulips pushing up here along the walkway couldn't lighten the mood.

This was his first, and he hoped only, trip to the Midwest. It had never been on any kind of "need to visit" list of his and Cynthia's. Their tastes ran more to old European cities, which they'd been visiting for the last five years, in the order of a negotiated preference— Paris, London, Seville, and the recently accessible Prague. They had been planning a trip for the fall that would include Rome, Florence, and Venice, but now he didn't know.

Kevin raised his hand twice to ring the bell, but lacked the conviction to press it. He was startled when the door suddenly opened and a young woman in a dark suit and thick braids barreled out and brushed past him. He heard a faint and snarly "sorry" as she hurried away.

A middle-aged priest in a cassock stood at the door.

"Yes?" he said. "One moment please." He turned to speak to a couple who had just appeared behind him in the hall. A paunchy man in an ill-fitting sports jacket stood holding the arm of a thin, worried looking woman in a faded print dress. With them was a gangly, long-haired teenaged boy whose soft features resembled his mother's. The boy's hands were in the pockets of his pale corduroy pants as he looked out the door, past Kevin to an unknown point beyond. Kevin could hear some earnest murmuring from the priest, though he couldn't make out the content. However, the man, obviously the father, was speaking loudly enough.

"What does she mean he doesn't need fixing?" he said. "What does she know? Look at my son. You can see. I know you can. It's not . . . normal."

Kevin took a step back as the slender boy slipped out the door onto the porch. For weeks, Kevin's internal world had been so dense he'd been unable to muster interest in anything beyond his immediate condition. He was curious now about this boy, whose distress was tangible as he watched his father through the door, rocking on his heels, seeming to teeter between attack and retreat.

The conversation inside increased in tempo and pitch. Kevin looked at the boy, who responded with a shrug, then withdrew his hands momentarily from his pockets and made a brief fluttering gesture that Kevin could not be certain didn't involve a middle finger. Before the hands disappeared back into the boy's pockets, Kevin saw his fingernails—finely manicured and ruby-polished. He flashed Kevin a sarcastic smile before glaring daggers at his father, who at that moment grabbed his wife by the arm and pushed past the priest and out the door.

The father didn't look at the boy, but said in his direction, "Let's go," as he strode down the walk toward the parking lot.

At the door, the priest tugged at his sleeves and turned toward the hall. He had apparently forgotten Kevin, who wondered if he, too, should just go. He took a deep breath instead and knocked on the edge of the open door to catch the priest's attention.

"I'm Kevin Saunders. I have an appointment."

"Ah, yes, I'm Father Hanson. Please come in."

The priest extended his hand for Kevin to shake and directed him toward a parlor with glass doors.

"I'm sorry, but you might have to wait just a bit. Please make yourself comfortable. There is a pot of coffee on the table in the corner and some cookies, I believe."

"Is this where . . . ?" Kevin began to ask.

"Oh, no. We have a private room for the healings. This is just where people wait if Genevieve is running late." The priest paused, then added, "She's actually not here at the moment. But she knew you were coming, so I'm sure she'll be back."

The coffee pot had been turned off, and what remained was pale and cold. There were no cookies. There was reading material, though, plenty, in the form of brochures about St. Timothy's—a stained glass window project, a new high school, and a proposed new lower school building. It also seemed that the church sponsored organized trips to Italy and Ireland every year. Each brochure included a pledge card. So this is how it works, he thought. I pick one of these projects, and my donation pays for "healing."

Kevin, whose memory of churches from his childhood was dim at best, wondered for the first time about the management of parishes and congregations. He had known that the Catholic Church was wealthy with art and property all over the world. But he didn't know or question how that money might trickle down to a small parish in the Midwest.

Kevin considered himself uncommitted in his beliefs, which

Cynthia had found amusing at first, then exasperating.

"So you're an agnostic," she'd said.

"No."

"Okay, you're an atheist," she'd countered.

"I haven't given it my full attention yet, so I can't fairly categorize myself as an agnostic or an atheist. At least not yet, but I'm not a believer in religion. That I know."

It was in the early days, and he'd been messing with her, though it summed up his feelings pretty well. The fact that he might have to start considering such things made him think more about Cynthia than religion. Commitment was often an undercurrent in their conversations, bubbling its way to the top in rare spurts. Before these last three weeks, he'd begun to consider a long life with Cynthia, though he hadn't yet told her. He moved slowly in some matters, as Cynthia was happy to tell him. All of that was submerged now in a haze of incredulity as he once again realized he was sitting in the parlor of a Catholic rectory in a viewless town that seemed like the deep hull of a ship blind to the seaboards on either side.

Cynthia herself was a Catholic of sorts, born and raised in it, but now participated in its practices only when it suited her—mostly Christmas high mass at the cathedral (she liked the music) and Easter (for the drama). She had no time for the Pope or the hierarchy of the church and had no wish to convert anyone—including Kevin. It was a client, the elderly Mrs. McNally, who had told Cynthia of a healer who was becoming an underground phenomenon. Apparently, she was a friend of some bishop in the know. Cynthia never let a good opportunity go unraked.

She'd come to his apartment a week ago, bursting through the door with an airline ticket and a hotel reservation in one hand, their Friday night take-out in the other, and a lot of passionate "face to the jury" exposition.

"I can't go with you," she'd said. "I have that big court case coming up. The ticket is for Thursday, and you have an appointment with her on Friday."

"Her?" Kevin had said.

Cynthia was a large presence in his small kitchen: tall and slender, with sleek brown hair and a courtroom power suit. The fact that she had spent the last few weeks researching treatments and doctors throughout the country had been standard "Cynthia the Competent" fare.

"Yes," Cynthia said, "she's a healer, a young woman, who has apparently cured people of cancer. It's all been a little bit hush-hush, but she does her work at a Catholic church in Iowa."

Kevin would have been amused, in other circumstances, by Cynthia's newfound faith in something she would have previously derided. He had heard plenty about one of her co-workers who easily succumbed to every new-age fad. But there'd been other changes in Cynthia since his diagnosis, and they stirred something deeper in Kevin. He was moved by her newfound tenderness. He'd grown used to the way she protected her sleep by isolating herself in bed with earplugs and eye covers, and was touched by the way she now fiercely spooned her body to his in bed at night. He liked it, but it sometimes made him wary, too, as if the purpose undermined the act.

An avid racquetball and tennis player, Kevin was not perceptibly sick, even to himself. Until recently, he'd held a healthy appreciation for his own looks, intelligence, and prospects. There had been an easy predictability with which his life had unfolded until this point—loving parents (who didn't make too many demands on him), good schools, a job he loved, and an impressive girlfriend. He'd had confidence. It was lost to him now.

"Cyn, really, I think I should just go with Dr. Brenner's plan," he said. He didn't think there was a girl in Iowa, or anywhere, who could heal him. But he needed to handle Cynthia.

At the table, Cynthia repeatedly flicked her finger over her thumb, a nervous habit he'd had to develop a tolerance for.

"Kevin, look, it won't hurt to try the healer. If it doesn't work, you've lost nothing more than a couple of days."

So here he was in the rectory waiting room, thirty minutes since Father Hanson had left him. It was time to find the priest; he followed the sound of talking, which led him to a closed door.

"When did she get back? No, please, you must let me speak to her. There is a gentleman who has come all the way from Philadelphia. He's waiting here right now."

There was a pause, then, "Testicular cancer." Then mostly silence for a few minutes, aside from an occasional weary, "But, but," from Father Hanson, as if he'd been through this conversation before.

At the sound of "testicular cancer," words Kevin still had a hard time repeating aloud, it dawned on him that this little adventure Cynthia had insisted on was over. It was nothing more than a distracting side trip on the way to his fate, for which there was no easy alternative. It would have to be exactly what his doctor recommended: surgery, chemotherapy, and whatever outcome awaited him. With Father Hanson still talking, Kevin walked softly down the hall toward the front door and left.

◇—◇—◇

"What was it like?" Cynthia asked as soon as Kevin picked up the phone in his hotel room that night.

He'd been asleep, though it was now only eight o'clock. Lately, he'd found that sleep came at odd moments. He hadn't remembered falling asleep, but here he was—fully dressed, on his back, one hand cupping his balls, jarred awake by the ring and into awareness by Cynthia's voice.

"It was like nothing. She was a no-show."

He felt Cynthia thinking as his dreams dissipated. He'd dreamt he was on a trip, and when he got to the hotel, his suitcase was empty. He thought there might have been another dream, too, about something else that was empty, but he couldn't catch the thread of it.

"But you can go back tomorrow, right?" Cynthia asked.

"Well, no. She appears to be AWOL at the moment. Really, Cyn, it was pretty weird at the church. I've got a good plan with the doctors, and I will be just fine." He was surprised by the confidence in his voice and sat up, holding it, hoping to mold his body to it.

"Marry me," he said. He hadn't known he was going to say that.

"What?"

"I know, I'm sorry, this isn't how I planned to do this."

"You were planning to propose?"

Kevin thought to himself, well, yes, although he hadn't realized it. He didn't share this with Cynthia.

"Yes, of course. I've just been waiting for the perfect time, and then all of this happened. So I decided this moment was the perfect time. Any moment should be the perfect time." The words tumbling out surprised him, and he observed them like a witness to an accident.

There were two sides to this cancer experience. Kevin's side, and the one he shared with Cynthia. His was an anxious fear of mortality and a visceral terror of emasculation. The other experience, the one he and Cynthia shared, was a series of interactive discussions and events that included doctors' appointments, hospital tests, infertility questions, side effects, and long-term effects.

Prior to this, they had not specifically talked about children, though Kevin figured they were in his future somehow, someday. Now everything was speeding up, condensing. The future and the past were combined, perhaps because the future would be short. Where had all those years gone? He was a software engineer who could lose days at a time working out a problem or building a system. His relationship with Cynthia had taken a few years to get off the ground because they'd each been so busy starting their careers. There'd been some persistent push-pull dynamic in their relationship. Cynthia pushed him, in many ways, and he regularly pulled back into himself or his work. They'd never even moved in together. She didn't like his bachelor apartment, and her place wasn't suitable to his erratic computing hours. They were ready now, he could see. But then cancer—or because of it.

Clarity was returning. From his bed, he could see himself in the dresser mirror as he spoke and felt the slippery heft of the bedspread beneath him.

"Maybe this isn't a good time to ask you. Let's wait and see how the surgery turns out," he said.

"No! I mean, yes, of course I'll marry you. I love you," Cynthia said. "No matter what. But you're going to have to do this whole proposal thing over again, you know that."

"Yes, I know." And that was it—one future sealed, the other undetermined.

"But first, look, I want you to stay there through tomorrow night. Let me see if I can do something," Cynthia said.

"There's nothing for you to do. Really." Kevin knew that no matter what he said, Cynthia would have her way, but he had to try.

"Kevin, listen to me. Stay one more night, or at least get a late flight for tomorrow. For me. For your fiancée. Wow, I'm your fiancée."

"Yes, you are. Okay, I'll stay."

◇—◇—◇

The following day, Kevin drove through yet another neighborhood of similar houses—mock colonials, split entries, ranches, all with the same beige brick façades—until he found the number that Cynthia had given him. It was not far from the church. Cynthia had told him to arrive at eleven. The family's name was Eriksson, and their daughter, Genevieve, was the supposed healer.

Kevin stood on the stoop and felt a familiar reluctance to ring the bell. He looked around at the yard of this suburban house. The morning sky had turned sunny, and there were crabapple trees in bloom and tulips in the narrow beds lining the walk. The attached garage sported a basketball rim, and there was a ball in the driveway next to a minivan. The house seemed so ordinary that Kevin worried he was at the wrong place. He rang the bell.

The door opened to reveal a woman with wavy auburn hair. She spoke to him through the glass storm door, which she latched before she asked, "Can I help you?"

"I'm Kevin Saunders." The woman waited. "I have an appointment."

The woman turned and called over her shoulder, "Bo?"

A tall blond man appeared next to the woman—her husband, he assumed. They were a good-looking couple in their mid-forties, even if they weren't friendly. The woman murmured something to her husband that Kevin couldn't hear behind the glass. Kevin looked again at the address he'd written on the hotel's stationery.

"Is this the Eriksson house?" he said.

"How did you get this address?" The answer was in the question. Kevin had stepped into another of Cynthia's pushes. It was obvious these people weren't expecting him. He turned to go. At this point, he didn't even feel like explaining. He wanted to go home, back to work, back to whatever awaited him at his doctor's office.

As he walked toward his car, the woman called, "Were you at the rectory yesterday?" He turned and nodded. She looked at her husband, who was shaking his head, then she looked at Kevin and said, "Please wait a minute."

Kevin took a few steps toward her just as she halfway shut the inner door. There was some hushed deliberation going on out of his sight. Kevin waited and watched two small children riding tricycles on the sidewalk across the street. He didn't want to be here, but he didn't feel he could leave while he was being discussed. He was irritated with Cynthia that she would send him here without an invitation, assuming it would work out. That was Cynthia's way: "Ask for forgiveness, not permission."

Finally, the door opened, and the woman invited him in. "I'm Sheila Eriksson, Genevieve's mom. I'm sorry about the mix-up. We have to be careful about who Genevieve meets. You understand." She almost smiled.

He didn't, but nodded anyway. All he knew was what Cynthia had told him. She'd made all the arrangements, and he had let her. He realized now that he had not asked many questions. He felt foolish, not for the first time these past two days. Sheila showed him into the living room, a comfortable family space with magazines and books on the table and a few dirty tennis socks that she grabbed before Kevin sat down.

"How much do you know about Genevieve?" Sheila asked. She sat on a chair across from Kevin.

"My girlfriend—well, she's my fiancée really—made the arrangements. I don't know much about all of this, sorry. I guess you know I have cancer."

She looked down at the socks in her hands, which she rolled and unrolled as she spoke. "You know, it's important you understand that Genevieve can't help everyone."

Kevin nodded. The situation was ridiculous. All this way for a disclaimer for something he'd never believed in, stuck here being polite to people who were clearly put out by his presence. His six o'clock flight could not come soon enough.

Bo returned with keys in his hand. "I called Father Hanson. Genuine left before you arrived yesterday?"

"Yes, I think so," Kevin said. "Genuine? I thought her name was Genevieve?"

"Genevieve is her Christian name," Sheila said as she shot her husband a glance.

"You're a friend of Edith McNally's," Bo said.

"My fiancée knows her; she's the one who arranged this."

Bo turned to his wife. "The boys' tennis match starts in twenty minutes. Are you going, or am I?"

Sheila looked at Kevin and then said to her husband, "No, you go. I'll stay here. Wish the boys good luck for me."

Kevin knew that Bo had said this for his benefit. He was driving home the interruption to their plans, their normal Saturday life.

"Really, this was a bad idea. I'm sorry. I think I should go." He started out of his seat.

"No, you should stay. Gen made a promise, and she has to keep it," Sheila said.

"She didn't promise anything," Bo said to his wife. "Father Hanson makes all her promises for her." Then he turned to Kevin and said, "I'm sorry, that was rude. You should stay. I've talked to Gen, and she'll be right down."

Bo left through the front door, and Kevin wished that he could walk out behind him. When he turned back to Sheila, hoping she would take care of the small talk for him, the girl from yesterday stood before him, the one who had rushed out of the rectory. The braids he had seen, pitch black to the waist. What he hadn't seen the day before was her face—unexpected, beautiful, with wide-set eyes and thick eyebrows. It was oddly unsettling to look at her. He could see that she was barely out of her teens, if that. The prim suit from the day before had been replaced with baggy jeans and an oversized flannel shirt, a look that he and Cynthia had often commented on and derided.

"Gen, don't you think you should change your clothes?" her mother asked.

"Dad said I was okay like this." Her tone was clearly impatient.

Kevin stood. He'd had enough; it was time to leave. The girl looked at him from head to toe. She was appraising him in some way, but he wasn't sure it had anything to do with his cancer.

She put out her hand. "Hi, I'm Genuine. I'm sorry I missed your appointment yesterday. There was some . . . stuff." She raised her eyebrows as if waiting for something. He realized he'd been staring, and her hand was still outstretched. He took it. A warm hand. It made him feel something; he wasn't sure what. He couldn't take his eyes away from her face, and she kept holding his hand, so they stood there like that for a very long moment. He felt an embarrassing stirring in his groin, something he hadn't felt for weeks, and the impropriety of it appalled him. She was so young. But it was her face that flushed, though he couldn't imagine why.

"I'm Kevin Saunders. Thank you for seeing me. I have cancer." He felt like he'd just made an awkward confession at an AA meeting.

The girl held his hand a moment longer and said, "Hmm." She turned to her mother. "I think I should take him upstairs to my room."

Her mother's hands flew up out of her lap in objection. "Gen, I don't think that's a good idea."

The girl's eyebrows knitted together to form a line across her brow. "He needs some privacy, Mom. Give him a break."

Kevin glanced toward Sheila, who said, "You can use our room." And then, to Kevin, "I apologize for the mess. I wasn't expecting company."

Genuine took his hand again and said, "C'mon." He felt awkward being led by her up the stairs. He thought of Cynthia—what she would say about this and how he was angry with her for putting him here. At the top of the stairs, the girl led him into a small room, obviously her own.

"My room is better," she said, still holding his hand as she pulled him through the doorway. He felt dizzy and a little disoriented, as if he'd climbed more than a few stairs and arrived at an unknown destination.

In the bedroom, Genuine had him sit on the bed while she sat facing him in a desk chair. He wasn't sure if her room looked like a normal teen's room. He didn't have sisters, and Cynthia's place had always been one of arch decor and obsessive tidiness. There was a full bookshelf, a desk with more books, a large CD player, and some clothes hanging on the back of the closet door. Gustav Klimt's *The Kiss*, Botticelli's *Birth of Venus*, a series of religious-looking prints, and a black-and-white photo of Frida Kahlo hung around the room. He noticed, then, the similarity in Genuine's eyebrows. He had always been a little repulsed by Kahlo's looks, but it was not the same with this girl. The hair and brows were disarming.

Kevin stood up. "Look, your mother told me you might not be able to help, and really, that's fine. I made a mistake coming here. My girlfriend arranged this, and now I need to go. I have a plane to catch." Though this was not entirely untrue, he felt improbably guilty for the bit of a lie it was.

She looked him up and down again. There was not anything particularly provocative in the look, more like simple curiosity. She said, "I think I can help. It won't take too long."

Kevin looked about the room and then down at Genuine. He was six foot four and felt uncomfortable towering over the girl. He sat on the bed again.

"What do you do for a living?" Genuine asked.

"I'm a software engineer. I'm a partner in my own company."

"Do you like it?"

Of all the things that Kevin might have expected from a healer, which wasn't really much of anything, it wasn't being questioned this way. He felt like he was being interviewed for a job.

"Yes, I do like it," he said.

Then the girl went on to ask him more questions.

Where did he live? Philadelphia.

What kind of music did he like? All kinds of rock.

Did he have siblings? Yes, one brother.

Were his parents still alive? Yes, though he wondered how old she thought he was.

Where did he go to college? Did he like it? Did he live in the dorms when he was there?

Was he religious? He was wary here, because he wasn't sure how to answer. He shrugged and said, "Does it matter to the healing?"

There was a knock on the door. Sheila poked her head in and said, "I thought you were going to use my room."

The girl looked at her mother briefly, then turned back to Kevin as she said, "This is better."

Sheila gave Genuine a worried look and then cast a glance toward

Kevin, who felt embarrassed to be sitting on the bed, though there was no other surface available but the floor.

"Are you almost done?"

Genuine screwed up the side of her mouth and shrugged. "It might take a while longer."

Sheila pulled the door but left it slightly ajar, and Kevin noticed another art print there. It was a Madonna holding a naked Christ child in her lap while odd torso-less cherubs hovered with a crown above her head.

"Dürer," she said.

"What?"

"That's an Albrecht Dürer. Print of course."

Now they were talking art? Well, perhaps she would forget the question about religion. He turned to the wall behind him and noticed that the series of religious prints were all Renaissance Madonnas, each with either a naked child or a bare-breasted nursing woman.

"I see you like Madonna paintings," he said.

Genuine clasped her hands together and stretched them inside out in front of her.

"I like the Renaissance, but of the Madonnas, I only like these particular ones. I'm supposed to go to Rome this summer with my mother and Father Hanson. I want to go to Florence to see Michelangelo's *David*, but Father Hanson isn't sure we'll have time."

"What are you doing in Rome?" Kevin asked.

She kicked off her shoes, pulled the desk chair closer to him, and put her feet up on the bed. He couldn't tell what kind of body she had under the baggy clothes.

"We're supposed to see the pope."

"Because of your healing abilities?" Kevin surprised himself. If he were asked, he would have to say that he had no belief in this girl's ability.

"Yes." She looked around the room as if distracted by something.

Then she stood and took off her shirt. Kevin was on his feet at the second button, but the girl laughed and said, "Don't worry, I'm just hot."

Underneath the flannel shirt, she had on a t-shirt. It had long sleeves, but the front scooped just low enough.

"Please, sit," she said.

"How old are you? Do you mind me asking?"

"No, I don't mind, but it's not important to know."

He was at a loss for where to go from here. He finally asked, "Can you heal me?" Perhaps best to get the elephant out of the room. Bring the whole thing to a close.

"I already did," Genuine said.

He thought of Cynthia and the times early on when she'd played elaborate practical jokes on him as bids for his attention. She couldn't possibly have done something like that again, not when so much was at stake. But it crossed his mind.

"When?" Kevin didn't believe it, of course, and he didn't know whom he was humoring—the girl or himself.

"When I shook your hand downstairs. But you'll need to come back again."

"I have a flight out today, and I need to get back to work." Kevin was done. Fed up. Ready to go.

"Well, you could come back in a few weeks," the girl said. "Go to your doctor first, see what he says. You can call me here at the house. Don't bother calling Father Hanson."

Genuine went over to the desk and wrote something. She handed him a small picture with her number on the back, brushing his hand with her fingertips, which he couldn't be sure was on purpose. It was a school photo of her in uniform, her braids wound up around her head, eyebrows relaxed and un-knitted. In her smile was a subtle, but unmistakable, invitation.

◊—◊—◊

Kevin's surgery was scheduled for the Friday after his trip to Des Moines. He and Cynthia had argued each day since he'd come home. She wanted him to have more tests to see if the girl had actually healed him. Kevin just wanted to get the surgery over with and get on with whatever came after that. Cynthia seemed to take his refusal personally, and Kevin was angry that she was asking him to delay. There was no talk of the engagement.

He didn't show the picture of Genuine to Cynthia. He should have, he knew. It might relieve her of her fantasies about the girl's healing powers, but he didn't want to talk about Genuine. Not with Cynthia. He put it in a drawer, under his socks.

When he woke still groggy from the surgery, there were three doctors standing at his bed, plus Cynthia. It must not have gone well, he thought. He worried that he had not yet told his parents, realizing now how hurt they would be. They lived in Virginia, and it wouldn't have been hard for them to come. His brother, David, lived even closer with his wife and two kids. He should have told him, too.

Cynthia was smiling—that was odd. She was saying something, something about being okay. Kevin was drifting and couldn't tell if he was awake or not. He fell into a dream about mermaids with black tentacles for hair.

A few hours later, he was alert and talking to Cynthia.

"There was no cancer?"

"No," she said, and Kevin could feel the restraint in her voice. He could tell she was trying her best to hold back an "I told you so." Then, "They still took out the testicle, though. They couldn't take a chance, but there was nothing in the biopsy. Everything else is intact. You can have a normal life. We can have a normal life."

Kevin figured he should be grateful, but the emerging pain in his groin distracted him.

"She said I needed to come back," he said.

"Who?"

"Genuine. The healer."

Cynthia's forehead furrowed. For the first time, Kevin noticed her eyebrows, always neatly plucked and arched. The thinness of them alarmed him. Perhaps it was the drugs.

"Sure," she said. But what he felt was the point of her mind drilling through him.

The Four Seasons

July 1997

His name was Randy—Randolph something the III—and he'd asked to meet us at the Four Seasons Hotel in Chicago. It was my first time doing this, this hotel healing. Kevin had arranged all of it. Randy was paying us a lot of money, and perhaps you might consider that a troubling detail, but I trust Kevin, and I know he has my best interests at heart. That makes it sound like it was his idea, which isn't wholly true. I am healing other people, too.

Some for money, some for free.

◇——◇——◇

I first saw him when we were checking in. The lobby was a wonder of marble and flowers and artwork. He gave his name as he registered, which got my attention. He wore a deep blue polo shirt with some ensignia that I didn't recognize, perfectly creased gray linen slacks, and smart, expensive-looking loafers. He was a decent-looking guy, not my type really. I would say too old for me, except for the fact that Kevin is too old for me (at least according to everyone but me). Randy looked like he belonged here—like this could be his home. He had quick and fluid movements, palming the room key and slipping it into his pants pocket like a magician with a quarter. He didn't look sick.

You might be surprised that someone with my ability would charge for my services, and I'm not saying I'm entirely unconflicted about it, but it's not like the church wasn't charging for my services in its own oblique way. My family has a few things to say about what I'm doing, each to their own agenda. My mother is worried for my body and my soul, my dad that I'm taking a year off from college, and my grandparents chiming in on all accounts, both about me running off with Kevin and also about how he's handling my career. But that's their generation speaking, as if I need a man to guide my life. Kevin's my partner in this, fully equal. And yes, this is a career. My career. I have a special ability; it's really no different than having an advanced degree and a profession. Despite everyone's concern, I'm pretty sure I know what I'm doing. Not to mention, I feel like I've lived a very long time. That's probably one reason I'm attracted to Kevin, because there are no young guys who have seen what I've seen and know what I know. I know that because I've tried a few.

The first client I saw that day was an infant. Kevin said I shouldn't refer to people as "patients" because it would give the impression that I'm a doctor. He said client is better; clients pay for services, and the service I give is the laying on of my hands. When I do, I can heal people of all kinds of illnesses, though not all the time. But one thing for sure is, once I touch a person, I can tell. People don't always understand. Kevin tells them, of course, there are no guarantees, but who wants to believe that? I know this from when I was healing people at the church.

There's usually no apparent reason, so I just assume it's something to do with the person who is sick.

The baby was a sweet little thing with wispy brown curls and skin like Belleek, the pale Irish china my grandmother likes. Her big eyes looked all around the room as she lay back in her mother's arms. She had a problem with her heart, a valve that had already been operated on, but it wasn't working, and she was due for another surgery. Her parents' expressions told me their story. There was love and worry and exhaustion. But between them, I could tell there was a pact that lived outside of little Melissa. No matter what, they would get through.

I'd told Kevin that I didn't want to know about who paid and who didn't, though I could tell from their clothes that they weren't wealthy. I have to set a standard for myself, separate myself from the business side of the healing. Kevin is perfect for this. He was a little reluctant at first, turning my ability into a business, but it made complete sense to me. The church had turned me into their business, so why not strike out on my own? You'd think performing healings at St. Timothy's would be the most selfless thing, but it didn't always work out like that. Father Hanson liked to stack the deck according to his favorite charity. I saw a lot of people who had more money than sickness.

Fortunately, things went well with little Melissa. Her parents were so grateful, and I was happy I could help her. I told them to check with their doctor, of course. But I know when it works. I felt like it was the beginning of a good day, a good year, and a good thing.

Randy showed up next, and I went back to the bedroom while he and Kevin finished their business. We both agreed that it's better for people to just see me during the healings. After a while, I heard the door to the suite shut. I opened the bedroom door. Randy was gone.

"Where'd he go?" I asked Kevin.

"He went to get his wife. She's the one who needs help."

"Huh, I didn't think he looked sick. What's wrong with his wife?"

"He said she'd been in an accident. She has a lot of bruising and an arm that's not healing well."

I don't see many broken bones, but I have healed them. The first time when Andrew fell off the swing set at home.

"Has she been to a doctor?" I asked. I had to assume she had. Sometimes there's ongoing nerve damage. That would be new for me.

There was a knock, so I started back toward the bedroom. I turned and looked at Kevin, who had his hand on the hotel door. He's so handsome. I got a rush of good feelings.

A moment later, Randy's wife, Claire, walked in. She was small and plain, with heavy brown hair and bangs that nearly covered her eyes, so I almost didn't notice the bruised and swollen one. She had on a long sweater, which was odd for the time of year, especially compared to how her husband was dressed. When I asked her to sit on the bed, she moved very slowly as if she were really sore. I don't know why, but I asked her to take her sweater off. Her right hand was swollen, and she had trouble with the buttons, so I offered to unbutton it for her.

She didn't say much while I did this; she just kept looking at me with an expression I've gotten pretty used to. Curiosity and disbelief and a little awe all rolled into one. There might have been fear there, too.

Under her sweater, she had on one of those little baby doll dresses everyone's wearing. I could see why she wore a sweater over it—her clavicle was swollen. The bruising traveled downward, disappeared under the bodice of the dress, reappeared on her upper right arm below the short sleeve, and vined on down to the bumps on her swollen hand. I was standing over her, and as she looked up at me, I could see some pale green and yellow around her nose, like a dull piece of abalone, but it was either fading or she had done a good job with her makeup. Her nose was crooked at the midline.

"You weren't in an accident, were you?" I asked Claire. I'm not sure why I said that, but once I did, I knew it was the right thing to ask.

She tried to look away, but I'm tall, and I was still standing over her. She was little, so it was hard for her to avoid me. Her eyes welled up, and she looked at the door to the other part of the suite behind me as if it were the gate to hell.

So here was something new for me. Of course I've heard about spousal abuse, and I'd probably seen something on TV, but I had never seen it in the flesh—the swollen, purple, broken flesh. Healing at St. Timothy's was straightforward, and I think that most people would have been too intimidated to do something quite this bold, bringing a battered wife to a church rectory. But, there was one family who wanted me to cure their son of being gay. That was about the last straw between me and Father Hanson, although he never let anyone like that get through again.

I asked Claire to wait a moment. I went toward the door.

"No, please don't say anything." She was so scared she nearly choked on these words.

She sat for a minute while I thought about what to do.

"We have a big event to go to tomorrow night," she said with expectation, as if it had something to do with me.

I looked around the room at the pale neutral tones of the bed-spread and drapes, the soft linens, and the sliver of marble floor I could see through the bathroom door. Luxury was the only word to describe it.

I went to Italy with my mother the year before last, where there was so much beauty. Luxury is something different; luxury is carefully manufactured beauty—not wrought from someone's creative genius or coaxed into being through divine inspiration. It isn't centuries of artistic sensibilities bred into generation after generation of families who know beauty as a certain provenance of life and nature. Luxury is for people who have too much money and no inspiration. Luxury is for people who beat their wives and wear fancy slacks. Luxury is paying someone a lot of money to fix the damage you've done before you take your wife back out in public.

I'm a healer. I don't pick and choose when it works and doesn't. But this. I went to the door and cracked it open. Randy was sitting with Kevin. I glanced back at Claire and motioned for her to stay. I went through the door.

"It's going to be more difficult than I thought." Kevin looked at me, a bit confused, but he caught something in my expression.

"But you can fix her, can't you?" Randy began to stand.

I motioned for him to sit down and said, "Kevin, could I see you in the other room, please?"

I stopped Kevin just inside the door and pinned him close to me so that Claire couldn't hear.

"He beat her."

"What?" Kevin said.

"There was no accident; he beat her."

Kevin looked over my shoulder, and then he got a deflated look on his face. I could see what he was thinking, that he'd gotten me into something other than what was planned. He'd helped me escape from the clutches of Father Hanson only to deliver me into this darkness. I felt sorry for Kevin. He'd had no idea.

"I'll tell him you can't heal her. I'll give him his money back."

That was Kevin, always doing the right thing.

But I said, "No. Charge him double."

"No, Gen. I don't think we should get involved. She needs professional help."

There was a dull sadness in his eyes as he looked over my shoulder at Claire. I don't know if he felt worse for Claire or for us, being in this strange predicament our first day out as a team. As Kevin was learning, I can kind of get stuck on an idea when I set my mind to it. I just said, "Charge him double," and opened the door for him to leave.

I glanced at Claire. She was starting to get up. "No, please, don't bother. Just tell him you can't do it."

"It will be okay, Claire. You need to trust me." I'd felt the heat; I knew I could fix her.

There was some discussion in the other room while Kevin broke the news. I could hear a slight rise in tone for a short time, and then things quieted down. I'm learning things about Kevin, too. He can be very calm, diplomatic, and logical. I saw him this way with my parents, though he wasn't as effective with my mom.

I tended to Claire. Healing is still a bit of a mystery to me, even after all these years. I learn things nearly every time. Sometimes, the healing itself tires me. Other times, I get the most amazing energy boost. But every time, when it's working, I get warm all over, my cheeks flush, and it creates a sensation that makes me feel as if I am a tingling transparent beam of light that travels to whatever needs to be lit. Occasionally the other person can feel it, too. That's how it was with Claire, although I've healed lots of people who didn't feel much more than the heat from my hands. For a few minutes, all the fear and anxiety left her face. She was quite pretty then.

Randy about peed himself when he saw his wife standing there without her sweater on. Her nose looked much better with most of the swelling gone. Her clavicle and hand looked normal now, not out of line. Some of the bruises would take a little while to completely clear, but there was always makeup. He fussed and petted his wife as if she were his most prized possession. Well, I suppose the idea of possession was the whole point. I guess I learned something else, too.

"Randy, could I see you for a minute? Privately?"

"Gen," Kevin said, "I don't think . . ."

But I'd already taken Randy's arm and led him into the bedroom. I motioned for him to sit down, and he obeyed.

"Nice pants," I said. I just couldn't help myself.

He looked down and said, "Thanks." But it sounded like, "I know." "And thank you for healing Claire. Poor thing, that accident was so terrible."

I didn't have a plan at this point. I realized what a big mistake that was. There was no way I could confront him; it would probably only hurt Claire in the long run. Who knew how I might set him off. I could be flat on the floor before Kevin could get to me. I'm not invincible, and healing myself, well, that might be tricky and uncertain.

I took his hand. The heat was there, and I could tell he could feel it, too. I don't usually need to find people's diseases in them; the healing just kind of works on its own. However, there are times when I get pictures of something happening in people's bodies. I wondered if what I was feeling had to do with his anger or rage, because it was my first time with a wife-beater. But as the moments passed, I knew it was something different. It was cancer in his pancreas. That picture came pretty clear. Just then, my hand went cold.

"Well," I said, "it was nice to meet you both. Take good care of Claire now."

Randy stood, a bit confused, but he just nodded and left the room. I stayed there until after they left, and when Kevin came back to the room he asked, "What did you do to him?"

"Nothing," I said.

At least that's what I still tell myself, over and over. It was cold, so I pulled my hand away. The healing works or it doesn't. But I don't get to decide. It's not up to me. No matter where this ability came from, god or demon, that's how it is. I don't decide. It was cold, I tell myself again. That's why I pulled away.

Lillian Walsh

June 1998

"This is crazy," Fred said, his jaw tense. He had a strong jaw: well-defined, attractive when he was young, and not unattractive now, but the look of it had come to mean something else to her.

"Perhaps," Lillian said, "but it's my decision." That was really an incorrect term. "It's my choice," she said. He wouldn't understand the difference.

"So you keep telling me."

"And my own money." It was all that remained of her parents' estate: a fund that had been in her name only, and one that Fred insisted she keep for her own use. She didn't need to tell him this—they'd been over it many times. He would have given her the money if she'd asked, and it wasn't about evening some score either. She was convinced of that, though there might be some later. Later, she thought. A hopeful word. He got up and walked out of the kitchen. They were at the end of dinner, just the two of them.

When the children were young, they'd eaten all but breakfast in the dining room. It had been her preference at first—she liked the view of the orchard, but he'd said, "Don't you think it's too much trouble?" Then in time, when she was busy and realized that dining room dinners didn't go far toward any kind of idyllic imaginings she might have had, he found an objection to dinners in the kitchen, as if the dining room had been his idea. He felt that she shouldn't be so busy. She knew that. She'd acquiesced. It didn't seem important enough. However, things were different now. She was ill; she could get away with a lot.

$$\diamond\!\!-\!\!\langle\rangle\!\!-\!\!\diamond$$

Kevin and I flew into San Diego on a wave of white tufty clouds after having passed over brown desert hills. This was my first trip to the West Coast. I've been to Italy once with my mother, but no other place out of the Midwest so far. In a split moment, the clouds opened up, and the blue-green harbor glistened like jewels in the water. It looked too shimmery to be real, like a mirage or one of those 3D postcards.

"It's so pretty, it almost looks fake," I said. Kevin had his hand on my upper arm, the soft underside, his fingers reaching up under my short sleeve as he leaned over me to look out the window, but the plane banked and turned away. In moments, we'd landed, and the little surge and break after the wheels hit make something lurch inside me. I didn't remember this from the landing in Rome.

"Are you worried about the healing?" he asked. I'd been frowning, but it was because of the lurching. He worries for me; that is, he does whatever worrying I might need to do but don't. It's a good arrangement. The plane rolled along toward the gate, patiently, unhurriedly— as if to slow time, to get us adjusted to the two gained hours, to let us know that even though we raced to get here, we needed to realign ourselves. A man across the aisle fidgeted, impatiently, wanting to release the seatbelt. But we'd been warned. Wait.

I said to Kevin, "Oh yes," and then I leaned in a bit toward him and slid my hand up the inside of his thigh.

He laughed, that slight exhaling thing he does, as if he'd just realized something good, and it's taken him by surprise. I feel that way myself, too, with him. And I do worry about some things—my family, and from time to time, my soul. But I haven't told Kevin. Not yet. I'm good at keeping secrets.

"Let's just go right to the Walshes'," I said.

"We're not due until tomorrow. I think it's better if we—you—get some rest first."

"I think everything will be fine," I said. I didn't believe or disbelieve. I just wanted to get on with it.

"Let's stick to the plan," he said. Kevin is good at plans.

Fred's wife, Lillian, was going to die from lymphoma, a disease the doctors had failed to cure with so many rounds of chemotherapy. Dr. Henry Patterson, his good friend, had recommended a bone marrow transplant.

"It's her only chance, really," he'd told Fred. "We can hit it hard, then replace her bone marrow."

Fred had not expected to lose Lillian this way, so early in their years. He wasn't even retired, nor ready to be. True, she had been tethered to him by an uncomfortably elastic connection, always pulling in and pushing away, at least in her mind and heart. With regards to her body, he believed she had always been faithful. But he was tethered, too, and could not conceive of a life without her. He could not envision the aloneness. Their two children lived far away and were starting their own families.

Lillian had recovered somewhat from the chemo, but the scans told the story of its failure.

"I can call and talk to her," Henry had offered.

But Henry hadn't called Lillian; he'd had his secretary call with an appointment time. Lillian was upset with Fred for that, though it wasn't really his fault. Still, they went together and listened. Henry took his time and laid out the course of treatment in detail. Lillian didn't say much until they got in the car.

"Absolutely not."

As Fred drove, an uncommon immobility took hold of his tongue. The longer the silence went on, the harder it was to speak. He kept his attention on the road, occasionally glancing in Lillian's direction only to get a glimpse of the back of her head. Whether she was watching the scenery zipping by or was overwhelmed by an interior state, he couldn't tell.

When they arrived home, she got out of the car and wandered off toward the orchards. Fred wanted to go after her but didn't want to run into Alejandro. Fred mostly didn't want his and Lillian's life laid bare to their gardener, though he suspected Lillian might do that on her own anyway. Alejandro's wife, Rosalba, had died of cancer a few years before, and Lillian had done a lot for the family at the time. Too much, he thought, always too much.

When she came in, she went directly to the bedroom. He followed.

"I need to lie down," she said.

"I'd like to lie down with you."

When she was going through the first rounds of chemo, he had hired a caretaker to drive her to her appointments and stay until he came home at night. He'd been busy at work. But today, no one was expecting him back at the office.

"Rosalba had a bone marrow transplant for her breast cancer," she told him. He knew that. Lillian had insisted they help Alejandro with the expenses. "I saw her in the isolation room. They'd put a stationary bike in there so she could get some exercise. She was there a whole month. Her skin and tongue were peeling. Her tongue! It was horrible, but she laughed about it. She was so brave."

Fred hadn't remembered that Lillian went to see Rosalba. Perhaps she hadn't told him. He held her now, both of them stretched out on top of the bed covers. He wanted to hold her this way for as long as he could, so this rare closeness would be the thing he remembered about her, blocking out all those ways she pulled away. She relaxed eventually, then he felt her fall asleep. He could reason with her later.

◇—◇—◇

"It's not that I want to die," she told him at dinner. "I just don't have it in me to do that. Even Henry said it's not a sure thing. I could die anyway."

Fred didn't know what had happened to his usual self. He'd always had plenty to say to Lillian, and she to him, but this was different. There was quietness to her resolve, as if she wore a sign around her neck saying "No Discussion." He made himself press on about the children, himself, and their needs over hers. It was mean, he knew, but he was desperate. He shouldn't have.

She cried—angry, bitter tears.

"I'm sorry. Lilly, I'm so sorry." He only called her Lilly in times like these, when he was on the defensive. She had been called this by her parents but had preferred to be called Lillian all of her adult life. He did it unconsciously, as if the diminutive form could cajole her into a forgiving mood.

In the following weeks, he had Henry call Lillian a few times, but she wouldn't budge. She was still feeling okay; the spots were growing but hadn't impeded any organ function yet. She had some noticeable nodes in her neck, and she took to being obsessed with them—how large they were getting. Fred could see a slight panic living under her skin, but she still wouldn't consider the treatment. He went to Alejandro.

"She needs distraction," Fred said. "Is there something in the garden that could occupy her?"

He was surprised by Alejandro's reaction. She hadn't told him the chemo had failed. When he'd explained, Alejandro stood still, and Fred had to leave when he saw tears brimming in Alejandro's eyes. Lillian's tears were bad enough.

Over the next few weeks, Alejandro did find some distractions for Lillian. He came to her with problems in the orchard, or a favorite rose that needed transplanting, or some aid planning the vegetable garden for the fall.

It helped some. Lillian seemed less nervous and jumpy—at least while in the garden—if not fully at peace. Fred suggested that she go get some massages, which she did. For a bit, she also went to church, a lot of different churches. Fred was put off by the idea of his wife God shopping; they'd been happy all these years going to the village Presbyterian church. Now on any given day, she'd announce that she was going to the Catholic church, or the Christian Science church, or the Unitarians. He let it go. He wanted her to be as happy as she could. Henry told him they'd have some rough days ahead.

He didn't know when or where she'd found out about this healer; she wouldn't tell him. The healer had apparently cured people of cancer. She didn't ask for his advice—it was a fait accompli—already paid for. The woman with the weird name was on her way in a few days, with her manager of all things, before he'd heard a word. He couldn't keep quiet about this.

"Ten thousand dollars?"

"It's my money."

Fred knew that the cancer could cause tumors in Lillian's brain and wondered if he should call Henry. He'd never heard of anything so outrageous.

She knew him too well, because she said, "Do not call Henry about this." And then, "I don't want to die, and I don't want to go through that horrible treatment. Just let me try this."

"It won't work," he said. Of all the things that could be said about either of them, rational was right up at the top—at least when it came to matters of magical thinking. There were other ways, of course, that a wife could be irrational. This was different.

"There's nothing to lose by trying," she replied.

"Except a lot of money," he said, immediately regretting it.

"So what?" she said. She looked hurt and teary-eyed, but what he felt was her disdain.

Rightfully so, he supposed.

—◇—

They were expected at eleven. At twenty minutes to, the doorbell rang, and Lillian found Kevin and Genuine standing at her front door. Fred was on his way from work, though she'd tried to dissuade him from being there at all. She was glad to greet them first, to form her own opinion before Fred showed up to throw his contempt around. She hadn't really paid for this yet; she'd lied to Fred so he wouldn't talk her out of it.

Lillian was shocked to see how young the woman was. She was barely out of her teens. Kevin was older by a decade or two. Lillian brought them into the kitchen and made some tea. She was nervous and wanted to let this whole thing settle on her. Though she wanted to believe, it didn't matter to her whether she believed or not. She'd either live longer, or die sooner. She'd find out soon enough.

"My husband is a bit skeptical," Lillian said as she handed a check to Kevin. "Best if you take the check before he shows up."

Genuine sipped tea as if this were the most normal of occurrences. Kevin slid the check into a folder, from which he brought some papers.

"We always have clients sign a non-disclosure and a waiver of indemnity."

Lillian had been told this on the phone, but as she sat across from this strange couple, she started to feel what Fred had been saying all along. This was foolish; it couldn't be real. Waivers and non-disclosures? She remembered her Aunt Constance, who in her old age had given nearly all of her money away with absolutely no trepidation to a succession of hucksters who sold her their various wares of hope—oil wells, land in Hawaii, shares in non-existent movie productions, and finally, heaven.

"Perhaps I should wait for my husband after all," she said.

Genuine reached her hand across the table and took Lillian's, who was surprised at the warmth of it, as if it had been in the sun for a very long time, storing heat like a brick. She turned to Kevin and said, "We can do that later."

She stood and said to Lillian, "Is there somewhere—?" She was cut short by Fred entering the kitchen. He could sometimes arrive like a stealth bomb.

He introduced himself by saying, "You're early."

Kevin stood immediately and offered his hand. "I'm Kevin Saunders." He gestured toward the girl. "This is Genuine."

The girl's long ebony hair was thickly braided and wound at the nape of her neck. Tall and solidly built, everything about her said "strong." She wore a summer frock and sandals.

Genuine held out her hand to Fred. "I'm so pleased to meet you."

Feeling at a disadvantage in her seat, Lillian stood, too. So there they were, the four of them standing in the kitchen. She wanted to break this silence before Fred found his ground. Right or not, foolish or not, she decided she had to follow through with this. She knew now that she didn't believe, but she had to follow through.

She took Genuine's hand and said to Fred, "We're going to the bedroom." She turned quickly so she wouldn't lose her resolve, and Genuine followed her cue.

$$\diamond\!\!-\!\!\langle\rangle\!\!-\!\!\diamond$$

I knew I could heal her as soon as I took her hand in the kitchen; that's how it works. The energy starts to flow, and I can feel that it's hitting its mark. But I like to have privacy if I can, because it's good for the client. I figured in this big house, Lillian would let me go lie down in a room if I needed to recover, which happens sometimes. I didn't want Kevin to know.

Lillian had been sick for a few years, the cancer growing here and there. A healing like this can take a bit longer than an injury that's just happened, though it's not often that I'm around for such a thing. The whole process keeps changing anyway. I never know what to expect. Sometimes it really surprises me how fast it works.

It took less than an hour to heal Lillian, and I didn't feel unduly tired, but I wanted to spend a little more time and be sure that her husband wouldn't upset her. I told her to lie down for a while, and I would be back to get her so we could actually have our tea.

I went to the kitchen, and I could tell right away that it hadn't been fun for Kevin.

"Your wife is going to be fine," I said to Fred.

"Is that so?" he said through a jaw so tightly clamped, it could have been wired.

"Lillian's resting, but you can go see her," I said. "Perhaps Kevin and I could walk around your garden while we wait?" I'd never seen an orange grove up close. The lushness of it all was astounding.

"Let me call Alejandro; he'll show you around."

We followed Alejandro down to the barn to get the truck and drive to the other side of the property to see the oranges. He said there were ten acres.

"Fred doesn't trust us," I said under my breath.

"He wouldn't sign the agreements," Kevin said. "Perhaps you should have waited before healing her." Kevin was good this way, using "perhaps" to not seem like he was giving me orders.

"It's okay. I trust Lillian. She'll make sure they're signed."

"You just met her. How can you trust her?"

"I healed her," I said. He squeezed my elbow. It's a regular thing he does, this affectionate squeeze, like he's reminding himself that he's here, that he's a part of all this.

When we arrived at the barn, I suggested to Alejandro that we walk, but he said he had some equipment to bring out to the orchard.

"Kevin and I can walk, and we can follow where you're going."

"Please, señorita, Señor Walsh would not like it." Then he looked at Kevin and back to me and said, "Señora."

I didn't bother explaining. People don't quite know what to make of us, since Kevin's obviously older than me, and we aren't married.

"Okay, Alejandro, let's not make Señor Walsh angry," I said. Kevin raised an eyebrow at me. I guess I was being a bit facetious.

We had some Valencia oranges off the tree. Alejandro told us about the orchards: the lemons, oranges, and limes. You could tell he felt ownership; they were his as much as they were the Walshes', though he mentioned Señora Lillian quite a bit. He busied himself with a piece of equipment, and Kevin and I wandered between the rows. I felt giddy with the pervasive perfume of the fruit.

"It's really beautiful, isn't it, Kevin?" I'd backed him up against a tree. He looked over his shoulder, watching for Alejandro, extricating himself as he did.

"You are," he said.

We meandered around a bit more. The sun was warm but not overbearing. A complete lack of humidity, too. A perfectly pleasant day.

"Let's go back," Kevin said after a while. "They might be worrying about us."

Alejandro drove us up to the front door. He had a basket in the back with some flowers and oranges, and he brought them to the door while we waited to be let in.

Lillian answered the door. She seemed flushed, but otherwise okay. As she stood aside for us to come in, I could see her attention was past us and on Alejandro. They had a quiet conference for a moment while she took the basket.

$$\diamond\!\!-\!\!\diamond\!\!-\!\!\diamond$$

Lillian carried the basket to the kitchen and offered tea to Kevin and Genuine. "I'd like to do that," Genuine said, "if you show me where things are."

Lillian looked at Genuine and wondered what it would be like to be her—so young and mysterious. In their early days, Fred used to tell her she was mysterious. She didn't think she had been. He'd just had a hard time figuring her out.

"I have everything," she said. "There's no need."

Genuine came anyway, carrying cups and plates to the table. "How do you feel?" she asked.

"I'm not sure I feel anything. Hopeful, maybe." Truth was, she did feel something, but she didn't trust it. She didn't know if she was reacting to Fred's tension or a desire to prove him wrong.

How do you talk about something like this? Something that might be nothing more than a sleight of hand that leaves another's hand cold as ice buried deep in the ground? Lillian didn't know what to say. She had felt the heat from this girl transfer into her body, and it bobbed around from here to there—in her neck, under her ribs, in places she imagined the tumors were growing. She had never considered herself a believer in magic. She didn't now either. But there had been something. Or maybe she had imagined something.

"Her lymph nodes are still swollen," Fred said, still driving his advantage.

"They'll start going down in a couple of days. I think if you wait a week for the scan, everything will be clear," Genuine said in the most matter-of-fact voice.

Lillian wouldn't have been surprised if she'd closed the sentence with, "and that's a fact." The girl had confidence—more confidence than even Fred was capable of. But there was also kindness.

"And you'll be well clear of here by that time, I presume," Fred said. Genuine looked at Kevin, her thick eyebrows rising.

"We need to get back," he said, but there was a question in the statement.

"We can stay," she said. "I'd like to be here for the scans."

"Gen," Kevin started but didn't continue. Lillian noticed a subtle motion of the girl's hand, her fingers really, as they lay next to her teacup. He had noticed, too, apparently.

Lillian wondered how a young girl could do that, what she had over this man that let her decide for them with such ease. Kevin didn't object, just nodded his head and sighed, but so very slightly. She had watched them from her window, watched them walk down to the barn after the "healing."

Fred had come and asked her why she wasn't resting and then started to barrage her with questions. She wanted him to be quiet. To just stand next to her while she stood at the window to watch the girl, the way she walked, the way she put her hand on her man, how she loosened her braid and let it fall down her back.

She wanted to know how the girl could go from doing what she did, here in the bedroom, to being so casual and normal outside as if it were nothing. Lillian supposed she was still trying to tease out the truth of what had happened here in the bedroom. But she had an interest in the couple, too. Fred kept talking. She tried to wave him away, but he'd persisted, and she shouted at him to get out. He'd gone somewhere in the house until they'd heard Alejandro's truck.

"You can stay in our little guest house if you like," Lillian said.

"Absolutely not," Fred said.

"She healed me," Kevin said.

"What?" Fred was caught off guard by this redirecting of the conversation.

"I had testicular cancer. Genuine healed me."

This would mean nothing to Fred, Lillian thought. Another card played in the hand of a confidence man, but it answered some of her questions. If it was true, Kevin was in Genuine's debt, so it was natural for him to acquiesce. It was not unlike her and Fred when they were young and just starting out. Fred had loved her, but he'd been in her debt, too. It was her parents' money that had helped buy this house, given them a place in the very closed society here, which allowed Fred to build his client base. He made a lot of money himself over the years, so that debt had diminished. She had been careful—no successful man liked to think that his life wasn't of his own making. But there had been a time when she should have recognized the kind of feeling this girl must have. The power had been there; she just hadn't known it.

There was something else, though, she observed with this girl and whatever power she did or didn't have. She looked at Kevin with a deep tenderness. She loved him back. Watching them, here at her table, passing the sugar or plate of cookies back and forth, Lillian felt the slightest twinge of jealousy. Perhaps this was just new love. New love's easy give-and-take. The absence of score keeping, the tabulations, the moments held back. All that might come later. She hoped not.

The couple took a hotel room in the village, visited a few times during the week, and waited until the scans showed her remission—just as Genuine had promised. Then they stayed a few days longer. Fred was chagrined, happy, and unusually tearful. He offered the guesthouse to them whenever they'd like. He signed the papers and swore to keep their secret.

On the days they visited, Genuine liked to walk around the property, learning the names of plants from Alejandro and taking obvious pleasure in eating oranges right off the tree. Kevin talked to Fred about investments and then made Fred even happier by asking his advice. On their last day together, they had lunch in the garden. Lillian arranged a basket of flowers for the table.

The couple seemed happy and relaxed. Genuine's faced glowed with the benefit of a week of California sun. She pointed to the wispy yellow poppies and said, "Eschscholzia californica."

Lillian smiled and nodded. There was nothing more to say.

◇——◇——◇

Fred told Henry that Lillian had been doing a lot of praying. Henry, who knew some things were inexplicable, expressed joy for his friends, though he warned of a possible relapse and the necessity to keep checking.

Lillian pondered what she'd do with her new life and promised herself to make things better with Fred, although she could tell that from his perspective, everything was quite all right. Perhaps just living was enough.

—◇—◇—◇—

Kevin and I were happy to be going home, though home is just an off-campus apartment for now. I would go back to school, and Kevin would go back to work. This was the deal I made with my dad. College first, then marriage. Healing when I could arrange it. Quietly. My dad didn't know, but that was already my plan. I am only twenty—I have a lot to learn about life. Near landing, quilted fields of corn and beans spread out before us like a welcome carpet. I reached for Kevin again, but he was ready this time, his hand already reaching for mine.

CC

August 1998

My mother always said that life is no more than a bunch of stories strung together. Sad stories, happy stories, weird unbelievable stories. She also said that by the end of one's life, a person's got one long yarn to tell. Some parts will be hard to tell, others not worth telling, and some just too crazy not to tell. I'm not at the end of my life by any means, but I've got a story that's just bursting to get out before my memory starts revising it.

Once upon a time, not a very long time ago, I was a paralegal at a law firm—Marks, Marks, Trumble, and Davis. The firm started with my boss, Bill Marks. As soon as his wife had their first baby, he added the second Marks, just to make it sound like more than a one-man show, even though all three Marks babies ended up being girls. Not to say, of course, that they couldn't be lawyers, but . . . the truth is, watching those girls grow up, I didn't think a single one would have had enough gumption or smarts to get through law school. Whiny, asthmatic, and unexpectedly dull, in that order.

Funny thing about gene pools, you never know what's going to swim out of the pond. Bill's pretty smart himself, and over the years he acquired partners and associates and turned his one-man show into a nice successful firm. Now, lo and behold, the youngest daughter, Liza, is in law school—not a big-name school, but law school nonetheless. I guess I have to revise my opinion, although I'm certain I wasn't the only one with doubts. She'll be lucky to come here to work, because there's no way she's going to end up in the top ten percent (or even the top half) of her class, which, as everyone knows, is necessary to get a job at a decent firm.

Well, back to my story. My name is Christine Champaign. My maiden name was Keller, and you'd think with a name like Champaign, I'd married up. It was more like a lateral move at best. I'm divorced now, but I kept the name because of my two kids, who, by the way, are all grown up, so in case you were wondering, this story isn't about them. And anyway, everyone calls me CC, a nickname Bill gave me when I first came to work here. He has a penchant for nicknames.

I like Bill. He's intelligent, as I've said. And, he's kept me on over the years, paid for night school so I could become a paralegal, took care of my divorce, and never said a word about my expanding size—though that wasn't the case for some of the snotty young associates. But I was good at my job, so that counts, too. Plus we had a thing for a bit back in the day.

Anyway, we saw all kinds of people in our office; really, all kinds. In addition to a number of corporate clients, we had the usual: divorce, taxes, real estate, wills and estate planning, malpractice, civil suit, some petty criminals, and perhaps one who was a bit more than petty.

Now, let me be clear: this is a story. I would never mention a client's name, and I will certainly change some of the details, just to be clear that there is no question of privilege.

(Wink, wink.)

One of the things I liked about this job is that we were always busy. I like busy. I like to blow through my day from one thing to the next. Recently, my day started with one of our regular clients who looks a bit like a daytime TV star or a young Efrem Zimbalist Jr. if you're old enough to remember him or have watched as many late-night reruns as I have. Classy-looking. Deep-set dark blue eyes. Very manly, starched shirts and perfectly pressed pants. Always has little monograms on one sleeve and always, always, wears French cuffs. Who wears French cuffs anymore? Well, Efrem does. I'll just use that name because it's easy.

His family had money, and he has some real estate holdings in the city, which, being Chicago, means he has money, too. Nice wife, a bit plainly dressed, but she's always very polite. Not Efrem, he's just one of those guys who likes to snap his fingers to get things done. He never did it to me, but I could tell. I can always tell about guys like this, as if I can hear their thoughts. Snap, snap.

Efrem, according to the word going around the office, was sick, and it's true he looked a little worse every time he came in. The wife never said much when she came to the office, kept her eyes down. I'd always tagged her as being brow-beaten. Women catch that stuff, particularly if you know the husband . . . all charm one minute, nipping your head off the next, then back to the smarmy charmy stuff. I pictured her at home doing some crazy thing like vacuuming straight lines in the carpet every night before Efrem got home, because you just know a guy like that, all tidy with every hair in place, would want lots of other things all tidy and in their places, too. I'm not saying Claire (oops, just a pseudonym) did that vacuuming, I'm just saying there was probably something. She always showed up in long-sleeved dresses or sweaters no matter the weather. Which I didn't really notice until she didn't.

Because of Efrem's illness, which I was fairly sure was going to be terminal, we'd been working on his estate, you know, planning trusts for the kids, etc. It was also clear that he wanted to tie things up so that Claire couldn't get to the principle, although she'd be comfortable enough if she sold their big house. Initially, Claire had seemed fine with all of this. Then she'd missed three appointments to sign the papers. But she finally showed up one absurdly busy Friday.

"I like your dress," I said. My eyes gravitated toward all that bare arm and clavicle. The dress was not immodest or anything. There was just so much more bare skin than I'd ever seen of her.

It was her tanned arms that attracted my attention the most. Thin and shaped in a way that you could tell there was a hint of muscle underneath—new muscle, newly worked. When I handed her a cup of coffee in the conference room, I could see the faint ridge of it along her forearm. Perhaps she'd been playing tennis or lifting weights. Then I noticed the bruises on the inside of her forearms, like someone had grabbed them both and squeezed until the thumbs left their mark.

"Thank you, CC," she said. She gave me a direct look, not quite challenging me, but as if she knew I had something else, something personal to her, on my mind.

Efrem, who'd been standing around while we waited for Bill, came up behind her chair and rubbed his hands up and down her arms.

"Claire, honey, aren't you cold without your sweater?"

The AC was running pretty high, that's true. I wasn't cold, but I could see that a little thing like Claire might be. I don't think she'd brought a sweater in with her. Claire didn't even look at him. She had her day planner in front of her and was ticking things off with a pencil.

"Where's Bill?" Efrem said. "I've got another meeting to get to." Then he turned to Claire. "We're getting this done today." All the honey he'd been oozing was suddenly stuffed back in the jar with the lid shut tight.

I noticed how gray Efrem was looking. Claire took an envelope out of her purse and said, "I'll be right back."

I went in search of Bill.

He was in another meeting with new clients. I could see them through the sidelight by his door. I knew his day was a bit full, but it wasn't up to me to manage him. My secretary days were long gone.

Bill saw me lurking and waved me in. "Oh, good, CC, glad you're here," he said, although he didn't look glad.

"The Efrems are waiting," I said, "both of them."

Things hadn't been going well for Bill at home for some time, and I knew all about it. I wasn't jealous that he was having an affair with the new associate, Jill. And I wasn't upset that Jill was a very skinny, very talented lawyer. Cute enough. But his wife, Emily, had found out. She'd found out about a few other indiscretions, too, although I'm fairly certain she didn't know about me. The way I look now, she probably wouldn't have believed it anyway. I'm not saying I don't know how she found out, but that's a different story altogether.

Anyway, Bill's developing one of those little baby beach balls around his midline, although he still looks good enough overall. No one would mistake him for a movie star, but I'm sure his looks are not what attracted Jill, believe me.

"CC?" I had been a little lost in thought. "I want you to meet the The Hoods. We are going to form a partnership for them, a charitable foundation, and we'll be writing some release documents and confidentiality agreements for their clients."

Of course I'm making up the names. The girl, I'll call her Maid Marian, was in her early twenties at most, and had the most amazing hair I'd ever seen, black, nearly blue black if the light caught it a certain way. It hung to her waist in a thick braid bound with a leather strand. She wore a longish floral summer frock, some chunky jewelry and lace-up leather sandals. The whole look said Renaissance fair. What goes around comes around, I'll tell you. She looked like an early version of myself, minus the hair and a few pounds. And the allure.

I struggled with my weight for a long time, and instead of losing, I just kept gaining. Diets and exercise would only last so long, and I finally figured out that if I wanted to eat comfort food, I'd have to be comfortable with my size. So that's how I am now, not hiding under caftans or in size twelve denial clothes with pieces of flesh poking out everywhere. I'll never resort to the lazy sweatpants look. I dress my body, big as it is, like the skinny girls do—with pride. I kind of admired Marian's flowy dress and wondered if it came in my size.

The man Robin, stood up and shook my hand. Maid Marian stood, too, and smiled, but didn't hold out her hand.

"CC, can you get started on those documents? You can take the The Hoods to your office while I finish up with this other meeting." There was ever the slightest bit of exasperation in his voice—not enough for the clients to notice, but I know Bill. I was pretty curious about our new clients, so I filed that bit of attitude away for another time.

There are all kinds of crazy people out there, you know, like the ones who want to sue the phone company for sending them weird messages in their dreams, or something similar. Or the not so unsettled but equally exasperating people who show up with a hundred pages of some brief they've written themselves about how ambulance sirens are ruining the fabric of civilized life. Every law firm gets a walk-in or two or three over the years like that. But this wasn't that. Not exactly.

Marian is a "healer." Okay, that's out there now. Apparently a real healer, as in she cures the sick, even people with cancer. Laying on of hands and the like. Works most of the time, she said, but not all, and that's why they needed some of our legal expertise. Robin's story was that they'd been running a little business, charging people for healing. They'd put together some boilerplate documents, but they were getting well-known enough that they wanted to cover their legal behinds. Good idea.

Now of course, there are all kinds of questions to ask. Are you kidding me? That might be the first question (although more politely phrased), and the answer was apparently no. Next question, how did you learn to do this? Well, it just came to her as a kid. Okay, well, I'm not sure stranger things have been true, but there was no comeback to that. I had a fleeting thought about the dying Efrem down the hall.

"Why do you charge money?"

"Why not?" she said.

"We've got to live," he said.

"How much do you charge?

"Depends on the circumstances," he said. "We've charged as much as ten thousand dollars."

Holy shit. Didn't say that, but my jaw was hanging.

"If it saves someone's life, why not?" was his response to my expression.

At this point, I gave Robbing Hood a slightly sharper look since he seemed to be taking over. She picked up on that and put her hand affectionately on his arm, so I didn't ask anything else.

"Okay, well, let's get down to business," I said. But from here on out, I had to wonder what Friar Tuck would say.

They were oddly likeable, weird story though they were. I liked the way her smile included her eyes, open and frank. Sharp, too. She had thought through all of the things they needed. They wanted to set up a charitable foundation to fund healings for people who couldn't afford to pay the asking price. Twenty-five percent of what they took in for healings would go to the foundation to provide travel for those who couldn't even afford the journey, whom she would then heal for free. The possibilities, if ever a thing could be true, were kind of mind-boggling. I said I was surprised that she wasn't really famous or something. I was just fishing.

"I don't really want to be famous. I'm still a college student."

Huh. Oh well, I thought, as I came back to reality, the kooks were paying by the hour. We wrote up some solid confidentiality agreements, even though everyone knows they are hard to enforce. No matter what you threaten, once the cat is out of the bag . . .

"We've been doing this for a couple of years already," Robin said. "Word has gotten out a bit, but the people she heals are really grateful, so that helps. However, we know the day will come."

Sure it will.

Right then, when I'd just written them off, I took another look and thought, what do I know? I got this little stab in my heart. You know, the kind that happens when you've got something buried deep, but some random thing will suddenly open that door again?

Like the way the smell of rhubarb pie can remind you of your long-dead grandmother? Well, the Hoods did that to me. I don't know whether it was their confidence or the way they looked at each other. My life seemed like such a small sliver at that moment.

When Bill was done with the Efrems, I tried to have a little chat with him about Marian and Robin.

"Well, that was interesting," I opened.

Bill didn't respond at first, just frowned. He looked a bit done in. Efrem can do that to you.

"You told her, didn't you?" he said.

I nodded. "The Hoods are coming back next Thursday. I told them the usual about the non-disclosures."

"No."

"Yes, I did." Bill was acting kind of weird.

"No," he said again. "You told her."

A little spider was crawling up my back, and I knew where it was going. But I stalled nonetheless.

"Maid Marian?" I asked.

"Claire," he said.

The spider went away. "Told Claire what?"

"That she'd be better off if she divorced Efrem."

Well, no, I hadn't, but it was true. She would be better off. "Is she really going to divorce him?"

"I don't think he'll live that long. But she's threatening a divorce if he tries to tie up the money."

"Good for her," I said.

Bill shot me one of those "thanks a lot" looks.

"He beats her," I said.

I looked at Bill and thought about my divorce from Mr. Sparkling Wine: Baxter. He'd told me so many things I never should have believed but did. He cheated, he lied, and he said he loved me—as the song goes. He also gambled, embezzled, and did some other horrible stuff. After Baxter, I wised up and took charge of my life.

Everything on my terms, Bill included. Baxter was the first and last person I'd let fool me like that.

"Emily, my wife," Bill said.

The spider started creeping again. I waited.

"You told her, didn't you?"

I used to think Bill wasn't your typical player. He didn't chase skirt out of any sense of entitlement. He was just one of those guys who was nice to everybody, and some of us naturally took it personally and returned the favor. Bill just let things happen in a charmingly passive way. He always went back home, and although she didn't play around, Emily had her own faults: all of it unpredictable. Lots of chaos theory ruled that relationship. But they kept it together. Life rolled on.

But then I'd found, on his messy desk that I tidy up from time to time, a file labeled "Emily." He had a range of documents ready for her to sign, some redistribution of investment accounts, some holdings to trust for the girls. The whole thing had the slick hand of Jill written all over it. She's a certified family attorney, which really means her specialty is divorce. I dug a little deeper and found a title to an apartment downtown that he'd recently bought.

He was pulling an Efrem on Emily, his wife of thirty years, for a skinny bitch who didn't care about him. She wasn't family. I was family; his partners were family. He was going to waste the whole thing and mess it all up. Stupid man. Stupid, lying, cheating man.

"I'm in love, CC," he said.

"I quit." I said.

I found a box, dumped all of my stuff in it, and got out of there before I had second thoughts. They were murderous thoughts, so it was good that I left.

Outside on the sidewalk, there were two couples having a pretty heated little discussion. It was the Hoods and the Efrems, although Claire stood a couple of feet away, gazing down the street. Evidently, they knew each other. My first instinct was to hang around to eavesdrop on that craziness, but my better instinct said to keep on walking.

The
Stone Wall
December 2005

The small cherub sat on a stone wall overlooking what had been the children's garden, now laden with snow. Milkweed pods poked through and stood shadowless against the dull winter sky. The statue, wound at the base with vines and spotted here and there with small clumps of snow and the detritus of long-decayed summer flowers, could not speak nor remember, but its countenance seemed mournful. Ironically this was the cherub the children had called their "happy angel."

Kate had placed it on the wall at the end of many months of dragging each stone from the end of the lengthy driveway to this spot, across from the kitchen, where she could have a view of the garden. Her husband had sometimes watched her while she loaded one heavy stone at a time into the wheelbarrow and pushed it the long distance to the plot beside the house. He had repeatedly offered to help, but she refused day after day. It became a thing between them all of its own, separate from that other thing—that ungrieveable event that marked their early marriage. That event was the reason for the wall.

It had been a long time ago and in the end, she had learned to grieve, and then to enjoy small pleasures, have more children, love her husband, and get on with her life. The stonework had made her body strong and capable, unlike the willowy delicate frame she'd been born with. It proved more useful to her this way, so even after the wall was finished, she'd found other hard labor and heavy lifting to do. Eventually she turned to exercise. Now in her sixties, the muscles and bones were still strong, although something within that framework was not.

She turned away from the window and back to the warm glow of the kitchen with its old fireplace. In the living room beyond, she saw the Christmas tree and presents underneath it. She could smell the narcissi that were blooming in pots all around the house. The house was ready. The children and grandchildren would arrive tomorrow, but other visitors were coming today.

"Are you ready, Kate?" Steven asked as he came into the kitchen and poured some coffee from the carafe. He stood at the counter in a yellow pullover and brown cord pants. She noticed that he seemed to have gotten just a bit shorter over the years. At seventy-two, he was always six years ahead of her. In the beginning, his being ahead of her had counted for education, but then she caught up. Then it had counted for experience, and she caught up to that, too. Now it was aging, and she was unsure if she would ever catch up.

He was handsome to her still, the once-young man who grew old alongside her. The sag around his chin, the deep chinks of wrinkles around his eyes, and the thinning gray hair on top were as much a part of the past as they were the present. She could tell he was worried about more than the outcome of the day. She understood his worry; he had his reasons. If he'd had to articulate his fears, he would not have been able to. But she could.

"Yes, Steven. Whatever happens, it will be fine," she said.

He frowned at her willingness to state what he believed to be unacceptable. He needed this cure more than she did, she guessed. What she had, the doctor had told her, did not usually have a "good outcome." True, at first she had felt very much like her body had betrayed her. All of those hard, capable muscles and the fitness she had cultivated had not prevented some other part of her from failing. Over the last two months, she had marveled at how well a sick body could feel, even though she knew that, right now, the small tenacious tumor was a mass of multiplying cells that would eventually despoil this feeling of wellness as it ravaged her organs. For the moment, she was not going to think about that. She was going to make Steven happy, see these visitors of his, and then she was going to celebrate Christmas with her children and grandchildren.

She knew that Steven had researched every possible cure, spoken with a dozen doctors, and gotten up in the middle of most nights to scour the Internet. He had always been an accomplished and able man. They lived in his family's third-generation home in Maine, where he, his father, and his grandfather had practiced law. Steven had fathered six children and seen her through the worst of adversities with fortitude and perplexed patience.

The doorbell rang, and Steven put his coffee down. Throughout their years together, as Steven aged, she could see reflections of each of their six children in him—an expression, the tilt of the chin, or a set of the mouth. It surprised her that as the children grew up and matured, different bits of them would reveal themselves in Steven's face. It was Terrence whom she saw in him now.

She stood, he took her hand, and they walked to the front door together.

Kate knew that in one of his increasingly desperate Internet searches, Steven had come across the name of Genuine Eriksson, a supposed healer. Kate's staunch Yankee husband had quickly grabbed at the straw of possibility. She saw there arose in him a kind of hope and faith that generally only comes when nothing normally relied upon will help, so what you never considered before must be the answer.

Kate had not felt the same hope, but she remained silent and let Steven have this moment. She loved him, and it gave him something to do until he was ready to accept what she had already considered to be the inevitable conclusion.

Steven had gone to great lengths to track down this woman who hid from people so that she wouldn't be barraged day and night with requests. Through many avenues and intermediaries, he had found her manager, Kevin, and made his plea in a way that had brought Genuine herself to the phone. She hadn't said much more than, "I'll come."

At the door, there were greetings and a short pause as the two couples took each other in.

Genuine was startlingly beautiful. Rich black hair hung down her back in three braids wound together. Kate had never seen anything like it. She thought she knew now why this woman would hide herself away, particularly if she really did have the gift that everyone claimed she did. Kate thought it was a shame, too, to have to hide such beauty.

Kevin was older than Genuine by perhaps fifteen years or so. He was dressed a lot like Steven, in cords and a sweater.

They went to sit in the living room to enjoy the fire and the way it warmed and lit the room.

"Well," Steven said, "would you like some coffee? We have sandwiches, if you're hungry."

"I'd love some coffee. Perhaps we could have a bite to eat after," Kevin said. He glanced toward Genuine. "Genuine would probably like to take Kate upstairs or someplace private."

"I'd like to be there if I could," Steven said.

Genuine put her hands on her knees. "I think I'd like to talk to Kate first, if that's all right with you."

Kate was surprised by the assuredness in the young woman's voice despite the deference in her remark. Steven looked hurt, as if he was about to be left behind by those going to a party. Kate put her hand on Steven's arm and said, "It's okay. Don't worry."

Kate considered Genuine; she could hardly not look at her. "We can go up to my bedroom if you like."

Genuine said, "I saw a small stone wall outside. Could you take me out to see it? Would you mind?"

It was an odd request, pricking at Kate's curiosity and arousing her out of passivity. This was really about her, after all. She could only nod.

Kate brought a blanket out to the wall, brushed off the remainder of snow, and doubled the blanket to make an insulated seat. It was cold, but there was no wind, and she was warm enough in her hat, coat, and gloves. Genuine sat next to her.

"This was my children's garden," she told Genuine. "I could watch them play from the kitchen." She didn't know why she was sharing this, but then she realized she was nervous. It was a feeling that she'd ignored since she'd gotten up that morning—some vague unease she had successfully disregarded.

From the low wall, they could see the kitchen window and a slight flickering of light that came from the fireplace. They were sitting next to the stone cherub.

"I built this little wall myself." She stroked her gloved hand over the surface.

"What was behind us, on the other side?" Genuine asked.

And there, Kate told the story, the one she repeated to herself in one form or another every day of her life.

◇—◇—◇

There was a pond on that side of the wall. Our first child, Jessamyn, loved to ice skate on it. It wasn't very deep, about three or four feet, but it was wide enough to skate around, and our winters are long enough that the ice was usually solid to the bottom. But one winter, when she was six, we'd had an unusual warm spell, and I'd told Jessamyn not to skate until we were sure the ice was solid again. She was a smart child—and willful. Our son, Terrence, was a toddler, not quite three. We just had the two of them at the time.

Jessamyn was in first grade. The bus would drop her off at the end of the driveway, and she would walk to the house from there. That day, I was inside with Terrence. He used to like to help me in the kitchen. He was standing on a chair with a spoon in some cookie dough, and we were rhyming and laughing. That was my favorite: the rhyming and laughing. It was about time for Jessamyn to be home, but I wasn't paying attention to the clock. Then Terrence said, "There's Jessie! Jessie's skating!" He waved at her from the window, but she didn't see him.

Jessamyn didn't have her skates on; she was in her galoshes, jumping up and down on the ice. I was furious and terrified. I took Terrence off the chair and ran outside. The temperature had dropped back down the night before, but I had told her not to go there because I had yet to check the ice. I yelled to her all the time I was running from the house. When I got to the pond, I screamed at her, and she stopped. She just stood there; her arms that had been waving about during the jumping were frozen out away from her sides. I checked myself then, realizing that my anger was overdone. As I looked at Jessie, I could see the widening of her eyes, not in fear of me, but fear of what she felt beneath her. In that one moment, that quiet moment as we looked at each other, she fell through the ice where the pond was deepest. I ran and fell through myself, although not to more than waist-deep. The cold was numbing.

I couldn't see her because the ice, as it collapsed, had caused her to fall back, and then it was around and on top of her in large pieces. I got to her, but she was unconscious. Her body felt frosted over, like the Snow Queen. It's odd that I remember that. I actually can't forget that, the image of the Snow Queen. I don't even know how we made it out of the pond. She had been in the middle, about thirty feet from the edge. I got her to the house and . . .

$$\diamond\!-\!\langle\rangle\!-\!\diamond$$

Genuine took Kate's hand and asked, "Jessie died?" Kate thought there was more than a question there, perhaps a perplexity.

Kate could feel the dampness seeping up through the blanket. She drew her shoulders up and put her head down so that as she spoke, it was as if it were to some inner part of herself.

"Jessamyn? No, I got her back to the house and stripped off her clothes and wrapped her in blankets in the living room. I turned her over and thumped her on the back, and she woke up coughing. I ran to the kitchen to call Steven to come home. I was still in my wet clothes and shaking with the cold. And there was Terrence on the kitchen floor, staring at the ceiling."

Genuine was holding Kate's hand and, even through the knit glove, Kate could feel some warmth coming from the other, ungloved hand.

"I saved one child and lost the other. Terrence must have climbed onto the counter to get a better view from the window. They told me later that the angle of his fall onto the old stone floor had probably killed him instantly."

Kate gazed off toward the kitchen window and said, "The details aren't so clear to me anymore. Well, some of the details. After we had the pond filled in, I built this wall to separate the spot and what it had caused back there from the garden here. I found the cherub at a yard sale. It reminded me of him."

Genuine stroked one of the stones next to her. To any observer, the wall would seem to have been built with care and considerable skill. Wider at the base, the stones were grouted only where some were too small to stay in place. The grouting was old and crumbling.

"Kate," Genuine said, "no mother could be blamed for saving one child and not the other."

"That's what everyone said. Steven, too. He never blamed me. Building the wall helped."

Genuine stood and looked at Kate. Kate could see that Genuine was thinking about what to say, and she was distracted again by the girl's beauty—her dark hair, the velvet blue of her eyes. It was an odd thing, the girl's looks and the idea of her "ability." She hadn't been that interested when Steven first talked about bringing her here.

She merely let him do it for his own sake. Now she was starting to wonder when it would all begin, and what it was.

As if in silent response to these thoughts, Genuine took Kate's other hand into hers, and again Kate could feel the warmth coming through her glove as she wondered if Genuine sensed what she was trying not to feel. She'd spent her life trying not to feel that she had been punished for the unspeakable act of loving one child more than the other, but that was the truth. She had loved Terrence more.

Kate sat, head bowed. Genuine stood and walked up and down the length of the wall. Finally, she stopped in front of her so that Kate had to look up.

"You're going to be okay," Genuine said, picking up the cherub.

Kate stood.

"But you need to take down the wall."

Arliss Eileen

May 2006

When I applied for this job, I was nervous as a tick in tweezers. I hadn't worked since I was pregnant with Georgie, three babies and a gazillion diapers ago. I drove around and around, looking for some road I'd never heard of, even though I've lived in Boone all my life. It's funny how some days stick in your mind and others leave like your brain was a drafty chimney. It was summer, and Ma offered to watch the kids until school started, although little Scooter wasn't going to school yet. I hadn't figured out what I'd do if I actually did get the job. It was disorienting to think of spending time away from the kids. Plus, I hadn't told my husband, Rusty, I was thinking of getting a job. There was no sense plunging into the subject with him until I actually had something in hand.

When we were first married and I was still pregnant with Georgie, he wouldn't let me work, even though we needed the money then, too. He was particularly opposed to me ever working as a housekeeper. Rusty's a mechanic at the Toyota dealer here in Boone, and though he had a scheme to open his own place, we were getting further and further behind on that plan. He was stressing over it all the time. He couldn't seem to understand that his stress ends up being my stress, so I thought I might try getting a job to reduce it for both of us. But no matter what, he always said he'd never want me to be anyone's maid. Except his, of course.

That day, I found the turnoff after a lot of mistakes, and it didn't help that the mountains were smoking because I had to slow down a lot where the wisps traveled across the road. When it rains, big drifts of fog hang, caught on the spindly tops of the fir trees until the sun gets hot enough to burn them off. It had rained for two days, and I didn't need the forecast to know that more was coming. The sky was loaded and ready to burst. The driveway, when I found it, was long and bumpy, gravel and dirt fighting each other to the reach the top layer after the rain. The only things I could see were the pines and spruces on either side and the long incline ahead.

My car's rear end was riding low to the ground, and I worried about leaving my muffler behind. Rusty would have given me hell over that, for sure—he'd been in a yearlong mood. I didn't need more of Rusty's hell, I can tell you, especially since the kids were still keeping me up at night in addition to running me around all day. God never told me that kids don't sleep. Well, He didn't tell me to have them either. You might be wondering, since my husband is a mechanic, why I worried about my muffler. Well, all I can say is, if Rusty was a shoemaker, we'd all be barefoot.

When I pulled up to what I thought was the end of the drive, there was nothing but a stand of firs in front of me. I thought I'd taken a wrong turn again. It would be a long way to back out because there certainly wasn't a place to turn around. But then I saw that the drive continued to the left. After another few hundred feet or so, there was the house. It was a big log house, and not like the ones you see in the catalogs. I'd been looking at those catalogs for years. Log homes are my daydream hobby. Rusty used to say that just keeping those catalogs around made him feel pressured. I told him that's not a bad thing.

The house had a stone foundation that came up to the first-floor windows, and there were logs on top of that. They were beautiful, no mold or tar oozing out, and a nice cherry color, too. I may live in a double-wide, but I know a lot about log homes.

There was a paved drive right in front of the house that led to paved parking by the garage on the left and more of the same on the right. I didn't see anyone, and I couldn't decide which way to go, so I just pulled right up to the front and got out.

I reached back into my car to get my bag and to wipe off my hands from the donut I'd had on the way over—the jelly-filled kind with the sugar dusted all over the outside. They were kind of an addiction for me, like people have with coffee. I must have taken a huge swing with my purse when I turned around because I nearly hit this man, who seemed to appear from nowhere. There he was with his hand held out to shake mine. He did this little sway away from my purse with his feet planted, kind of like those weighted blowup toys that kids have. I was so startled, I gave a little yelp. Oh, good. Way to go, Arliss, I thought.

"I didn't mean to startle you. I'm Kevin Saunders."

Tall, brown curly hair, and a dimple on one side when he smiles a particular way. Dignified looking, and maybe just a little younger than my dad.

"I'm Arliss Eileen Ford," I told him. I had to wipe my hand on my pant leg before I'd dare shake his.

He noticed that but just said, "Well, why don't we go in and look around?"

I had to take a minute to obsess over the massive front door. I paused just a bit for a closer look and asked, "This isn't a kit house, is it?"

"No, it isn't."

I could tell while we looked around that he wasn't much for small talk. I was prattling on, which is what I do, and he wasn't saying much. When I talked about the furnishings in the rooms or how I liked the view from a particular window, he didn't say a word. I started to think I was blowing my chance for the job, so I began talking about how I like to vacuum and how I think a clean house is just about one of life's best pleasures.

The real story is that I had big dreams to be the first one in my family to graduate from college. Hell, I was the first one to go to college. Never mind it was just long enough to get pregnant with Georgie. Rusty stayed and finished up his mechanic's training, got a job at Toyota, and well, here we are three kids later. And now I was applying for a job as a housekeeper.

I was walking around with this strange man wondering about how quiet the house was, aside from me talking. When I did stop to take a breath, you could have heard a pin drop—except I didn't. He walked me through all five bedrooms upstairs: some small, some big, all well-furnished with pretty lace curtains and nice beds with hand-made quilts, even one done up like a child's room.

I asked, "How many kids do you have?"

"We don't have kids."

"I guess you're planning, huh?" I don't know why I said that. My three kids showed up with no planning. I have a mouth that will run like a faucet, as Rusty likes to remind me. I couldn't tell whether Kevin was offended or amused. His mouth was kind of smiling in its crooked way, but his brows looked a little pinched. He didn't say anything.

One bedroom looked like it could double as an office of some kind. Except for that and the master, which was kind of a mess—half-unpacked boxes, things spilling out all over, as if someone was rummaging through each day for something to wear—the rest of the rooms were sort of unused-looking. It was hard not to think of what I'd do with all that space. I think I quit talking then.

Kevin was no longer smiling by the time we got to the kitchen. He went to the table and picked up some papers. The kitchen was something, too, big and open with doors to a terrace outside. Boxes were everywhere again. It didn't look like much had been unpacked.

"There are some things we need to discuss about the job."

Well, I knew it was for a housekeeper. That's why I applied. I figured

I was well-qualified, even if Rusty would think differently, but I wasn't expecting what he said next.

"We have a number of guests coming here, sometimes several a day. What we do is confidential, and you will need to sign a confidentiality agreement before we go any further."

I hadn't met any Mrs. Saunders yet, even though he always said "we" when talking about the house, and there was evidence of a woman in the bedroom—a few pieces of jewelry on the dresser and clothing thrown over the chair. But it was still just him, and it all started to seem a bit creepy to me, like this guy could be some kind of high-class drug dealer. My panic button started to whir up . . . you know, like a mosquito that's hovering but hasn't quite made it to your ear yet. He'd already told me on the phone what the pay was, and I have to say it was pretty good. More than double what I could get anywhere else. That was a plus. But that might also be the point: cash for silence. That buzzing got louder in my head, and that's when I started humming to myself. I'd let out about two notes when right up behind me I heard her.

"Kevin, let me take over from here." I jumped. I felt like running out of the house, but I turned. The first thing I saw was a mass of shiny black hair, wrapped and braided around her head with a single thick braid falling down her back. It could've been a wig, there was so much of it. I wondered what it would look like cut short. Maybe a porcupine, but there was nothing porcupine about her face. Her eyes were too wide-set for that, and even though I thought her eyebrows needed a good plucking, you couldn't call her anything but pretty.

"Hi. I'm Genuine." She wasn't local. He wasn't either for that matter. Her voice was a little on the deep side.

"Genuine what?" I said. I think having three little kids yammering at me all day just makes me blurt out whatever's in my head.

She didn't exactly smile, but there was a twinkling thing going on in her eyes. I wasn't sure if she might be laughing at me.

"Genuine Eriksson. And you are?"

"Arliss Eileen Ford."

"Arliss? Do you have a nickname?" she asked.

Well, the truth was my whole family called me Airless. My daddy's side of the family was all just a little bit hillbilly from Tennessee, and that's the way the sound came out of my grandmother's mouth when she first heard my name. It didn't help that her name was Alice, and she thought I should be named that, too. Also, I was a real scrawny baby, and my daddy had already said I looked like a deflated balloon, so "Airless" kind of stuck. It stuck again when I started having asthma attacks. Even though I've been trying all my life to get away from that nickname, Rusty also got into the act by saying that "Rusty and Airless Ford's Mechanic Shop" had a marketable ring to it. So I got to tacking on "Eileen" just to make it sound like I had a serious name, at least whenever I met someone new. All of this, for some reason I don't understand, I was in a crazy rush to tell this woman. But "woman" is kind of the wrong term. She wasn't much older than me, and I was still thinking of myself as a girl—a girl with kids.

"Well," she said, "how about if I just call you Arliss, and you can call me Gen."

We stood eye to eye, Gen and me. I'm five foot eight, and I guessed she was the same, although I weighed more. I said that was just fine, and by the way, I don't work for drug dealers.

"Well, Arliss, I don't think anyone should work for drug dealers."

I got to noticing that she didn't have a wedding ring, just a big silver band on her right hand that matched a silver cuff bracelet she had on. I looked around to see what had happened to Kevin and saw him rummaging through one of the boxes. He didn't have a ring on either.

"Kevin, could you pour some coffee for Arliss and me? I'll go over the papers with her." I hadn't even noticed that there was a coffee pot.

Kevin looked like he might want to say something, but he didn't. He just brought coffee cups over to the table and got a little matching pitcher of milk out of the fridge. It looked like some handmade stuff

I've seen over in Lenoir. Now that I looked around again, there was lots of that stuff, green pottery, and some other more colorful things in the upper kitchen cabinets, which all had glass doors. I thought about what a chore it was going to be keeping that glass clean. Personally, I like to have my kitchen stuff covered up. But maybe that's because it's kind of a jumble of hand-me-down junk. Also, it seemed odd that there were boxes everywhere and these dishes up there were all nicely displayed.

"Arliss, I know it seems unusual to ask you to sign an agreement before you even get the job."

That was one way to put it. She was sipping black coffee, and I was wondering how people could do that, without any sugar.

"I assure you that nothing we do here is illegal," Gen continued, "or even immoral for that matter. I think you'll understand once I tell you. And it's only for the purpose of this interview. If we offer you the job, there will be more of the same to sign."

Well, she caught me somewhere between that buzzing thing I had going on inside and a curiosity that would surely kill the cat. Just then, I felt something down around my ankles under the chair, and Jesus, it was a big black cat. Now, I don't think I'm the superstitious type, but I had just thought that thing about the cat and really, this place was out of the way and here they were all pretty and perfect and all. It was just too weird. I started to get out of the chair but didn't quite make it. I'm not airless-looking anymore. For a scrawny kid, I sure made it up to two hundred pounds in no time after I got married. I guess you'd think it was the donuts, but really, I knew it was the three kids in three years. I'm not saying I had given up on myself, but a lot had gotten away from me in those years.

Anyway, I was getting pretty wound up, and I felt like my asthma was going to kick in. My heart was pounding like it did sometimes, and my doctor had even wanted to give me some pills for that—antianxiety, he'd said. But I've never been one much for taking pills if I could help it, having had to take all that asthma stuff anyway. I told him he'd have anxiety, too, if he'd had three kids before he was twenty-one.

Right then, I was both trying to get out of the chair and trying to sit down and calm myself. I don't know what kind of crazy scenario was going through my head, but she just took my hand in hers, and I remember thinking, wow, she must have a fever. That hand was hot, let me tell you. And she kept holding mine, all the time talking to me.

Her face got this odd flush, like when somebody gets real embarrassed. But she just went right on, like it was completely normal to interview somebody while holding hands. I didn't know what was going to happen next, but I seemed to be getting myself under control.

"Arliss, what we do is a little unusual. Sick people come here, and I heal them. It doesn't always work, but it works enough that people hear about me and they come. Some pay us money; some have no money. It can get pretty crazy sometimes."

Crazy was all I could think. The only thing I knew about healers was from my friend Doty. She went to a revival meeting once, and the preacher healed all kinds of people—according to Doty anyway. She and I'd had a long talk about it. She said people were getting up out of wheelchairs and throwing away their crutches. She even saw a blind boy who got his sight back. I asked Doty what she'd got out of it, and she wouldn't tell me at first, but eventually she confessed that she could speak in tongues. I asked her to do it for me, which she did for about ten minutes.

All I could say was, "Huh," because all I could think was that she'd lost her marbles. Her voice got all pitchy, up and down, and whatever she was saying was gibberish to me. A few weeks later, I saw her with a black eye, and she told me she couldn't do the tongues thing anymore. Rusty, who I'd just started dating, said he imagined Mac, her poor-choice boyfriend at the time, beat the Jesus out of her. That was years ago when we had just started college.

I looked down at my hand. Genuine was still holding it and going on about what my duties would be and could she count on me. All I could say was, "I gotta go."

And she just said, real sweet-like, "Okay, Arliss."

$$\diamond\!\!-\!\!\diamond\!\!-\!\!\diamond$$

I ended up getting a job over in Blowing Rock at the Holiday Inn. The pay was lousy, but my mother was minding the kids. If I'd had to pay daycare rates, I may as well have just stayed at home and cleaned my own house. It took me a good thirty minutes to get over there, get parked, and hit the time clock at work. Rusty surprised me, said he liked the idea of me working, although I'm not sure what he thought I'd been doing all day at home with the kids. Things had been slow at Toyota, and there was no overtime to count on. Rusty's like that; he can change his position on a whim if it suits his needs. I never did tell him about the other job, the one I didn't get. Even though I never signed any papers, it seemed like too much trouble to get Rusty's opinions all over it. It might have been the first secret I ever kept from him.

After six weeks of cleaning up at the Holiday Inn, I was about ready to throw out all of my log cabin catalogs and resign myself to being poor forever. There are worse things than being poor—one of them is cleaning up people's personal messes in hotel rooms. There are so many ways people can be disgusting, let me tell you. High on that list involves condoms, and really, that's enough said.

All the time working at the Holiday Inn, I thought a lot about that big log house and what went on there. When you're pushing a vacuum, you have a lot of time to think. To tell the truth, I was thinking maybe I made a mistake. Maybe there wasn't anything weird going on, and maybe people thought Genuine could heal. Who am I to say she can't? I also know that I hadn't had a panic or asthma attack since I ran out of there that day, and while I certainly didn't think that had anything to do with her, it sure helped me think more calmly about the whole thing. But it was all too late, anyhow.

I was cooking supper one night, worrying over how I was going to tell Rusty there was no way I could keep working at that place. He was in the living room watching baseball with the kids playing on the floor in front of him when the phone rang. I had to yell at him to get it because I had the skillet going, and I knew that I'd just burn the whole supper if I went to get the phone.

"Air . . . Arliss, it's for you," he called from the other room. I'd been asking him not to call me Airless anymore. I liked the sound of my real name, and God knows, with the kids calling me Mama, and everyone else I know stuck in the past, I rarely got a chance to hear it.

I came to the edge of the kitchen with a potholder in one hand and a spatula in the other, trying to make it obvious I was too busy to talk.

"It's a Mr. Saunders," Rusty said. "Says he's calling about a job."

I went back. This time, I told Rusty straight-up I had an interview for a housekeeping job but nothing more. I just wanted to feel the situation out for myself. Even though the Holiday Inn was the worst place I ever wanted to work, having a job made me feel a little more in control of my destiny. I know that doesn't make much sense, but I wanted more of that, more control.

The house was kind of a mess when I got there. Genuine seemed a bit distracted, and Kevin seemed a little desperate. He was actually talkative. He said that they'd not been able to find anyone that Genuine liked, and they'd been pretty busy, so they were still not all unpacked. I asked him why they got such a big place, and he told me that the house had been built by a retired couple who wanted to open a B&B, but the husband had died unexpectedly, and the wife went to live with her daughter in Minnesota. Kevin and Gen had been hounded out of their other house, and this one turned up just in time, pretty much furnished, too. I asked if all that pretty pottery came with the house. Kevin said yes.

It was Friday, and I spent the whole afternoon there. For a while, we sat around and talked about the weather and Lake Watauga and the smoke in the mountains and all kinds of stuff, but not the healing. They didn't bring it up, and neither did I. I got to know their cat a bit better, too. Turns out he came with the house; the widow's daughter was allergic, so she asked Gen and Kevin to keep him.

"What's his name?"

"Pat," Kevin said and then laughed. "Pat the cat." Kevin can be funny.

I got up and started to unpack some of the boxes. It was just bugging me, even though I hadn't really taken the job yet. Kevin and Gen joined in, and we got everything put away, at least in the kitchen. Teamwork is kind of rare around my house. The kids are always working against me, of course, because they're kids. And Rusty, well, the teamwork he understands is something he watches on TV. I signed the agreement.

I told Rusty that I was going to work in a B&B, since it wasn't an outright lie. I just wasn't ready to get to the particulars with him, maybe because I didn't understand them yet myself.

I started the next week, and right off the bat, people were coming for "appointments." Kevin greeted me the first day and said that Gen was upstairs getting ready. I ran around picking things up out of the living room. Kevin helped, and I could see in the way he was swift with it that this was probably something he did regularly.

When I got that done and the entryway swept, I busied myself in the kitchen, all the while wondering what this whole thing was about. I was curious, sure, and I got to thinking about Doty again and her story about the preacher. I realized I never believed that the preacher had actually healed anyone. I found myself wondering about Kevin and Gen. They were so normal in some ways, and it was easy to believe they wouldn't be lying to me. But maybe I was being stupid. I wondered if I'd been tricked into being involved with something weird, although I couldn't imagine Gen speaking in tongues like Doty did. Still, I'd really only known them a couple of days.

Anyway, I was bringing the coffee and cups and all out to the living room when the doorbell rang. Kevin went to get it, but I could see out the front window that three big black SUVs had pulled up. You see these things around Boone sometimes when the summer people come. You know, the ones where all the windows are tinted real dark?

Well, here was a tall blonde woman with sunglasses on, dressed in black jeans and a long white sleeveless tunic thing with gold chains and bangles on each arm. She had a little girl with her, pale and bald but dressed up cute in bright prints. The girl looked about eight. It was a heartsickening sight just to look at a child that unwell. I don't know what I'd do if that were my child. There was a man, too. He was dressed like he was going to work at the governor's mansion or something: fancy suit and shoes with a gold watch. I saw that because the first thing he did was look at his watch.

"How long do you think this will take?" he asked Kevin.

"An hour or two. It's hard to say."

The man turned and spoke to some guy who'd been hanging around outside the open door. He motioned to someone in the other car, and then all three cars pulled around to the garage side.

Kevin had them come and sit in the living room. I went back to the kitchen, but I could hear (if I positioned myself close to the open door) everything that was said. I peeked out once just to check that they had enough cookies, but Kevin gave me a little wave off. The woman and girl were gone. They must have gone upstairs. The man was handing Kevin an envelope, and Kevin was passing some papers and a pen back to him.

The rest of the day, I was kept busy in the kitchen with coffee, more cookies, and some quick sandwiches for Kevin and Gen when there was a break in the visitors. They came all day long. They were even coming when I left to go home.

The rest of the day was a blur to me, but I will never forget that little bald girl coming down the stairs with her mama. Her mama was crying, and she kept trying to blot under her eyes with a tissue. I could tell she was going to lose the battle with her makeup, but the little girl looked like a different child. Her cheeks were rosy, and she nearly bounced down every step. She was still bald, of course, but anyone could see that she seemed better by more than just a bit. Even the father, Mr. Fancy Suit, looked shaken. They hugged Gen, and they even tried to hug Kevin, but he kind of slipped out of the way of that. Anyway, they got their bodyguards, or whatever they were, and took off right before the doorbell rang again.

This kept up for two more days—different people, different types, no more black SUVs. On the fourth day, Gen stayed in her room all morning, so I just cleaned and did laundry and such. Kevin sent me into town to stock up on groceries and more cookies and snacks for guests.

Later, when Gen came down for a late lunch, she had me sit and talk to her at the kitchen table. I do think it's my favorite room in the house, although there is something really peaceful about their family room, too, with the tall windows at the end that face into a stand of fir trees. The room has this real private feel to it, no TV in here, though they do have two, one in their bedroom and one in a cabinet in the living room. Kevin watches sports just like any other guy.

Gen looked a bit tired, which I mentioned, me having a big mouth and all. "It was a long day yesterday."

"Does it make you tired, what you do?" Until I said that, I don't think I actually *really* believed, even with that child looking better. I kept stuffing all that info away somewhere, not willing yet to say, yes, this lady's the real deal.

But now I was asking her about it as if it were the most natural thing. I guess that's when I started believing for real. From then on, in my mind, I could only think of her as Genuine.

"Sometimes," she said. "More so when I was younger." She didn't say anything more, just sipped her coffee.

"What does it feel like?" I couldn't help myself. Once I'd started, I wanted to know everything. All of a sudden, it seemed like my curiosity was bigger than anything, including my need for this job.

Genuine looked at me for a long while—at least it seemed like that. I figured she was trying to make up her mind whether to fire me right then or after I'd finished the laundry.

But then she started talking.

"It changes over time. When I was young, it was like having an uncontrollable magic power. I didn't know where it came from, and the fact is, I still don't. But it doesn't feel like magic anymore. It's just part of who I am. With a lot of healing, it's the same. I feel this heat traveling through my body, and the person getting healed can usually feel it, too, though not always, and whatever needs to get fixed, does. Recently I've healed without touching, but I had to be really close. Another time I healed someone over the phone, but I'm not sure that wasn't a fluke. People believe in the healing so much, I think they do it themselves. I'm still learning. I suspect I will always be learning."

Then I realized why I hadn't had an asthma or panic attack since early summer. The first time she held my hand, I thought she had a fever or something. She must have healed something in me. I wanted to ask her, but she kept on.

"And yes, I am tired today. I've been working three days in a row. Normally I like to work every other day, but it doesn't always work out like that."

"How many people did you heal yesterday?" I had left when the fourth appointment showed up. Gen had come down and told me to get going so I wouldn't be late for the kids.

"Well, seven people came, but I only healed six. It doesn't always work. If I add up all the people I see in a year, there's a problem with about twenty percent of them."

I wanted to ask what the problems were, but she looked away after that, and I just had a feeling not to go there. I wanted to ask about the money and about Kevin. But she got up and moved away, so I started bustling about the kitchen, hoping she'd forget how curious I was.

When it came time for me to leave, she said, "Arliss, you work here, and it's natural to be curious. I trust you not to repeat any of this."

I felt kind of mortified.

"I swear . . ."

She walked me to the door and held it open.

"I appreciate your confidentiality," she said. "I know it must be hard to keep this from your husband."

Well, she had that completely wrong. Rusty was so wrapped up in his business schemes that he didn't really ask me much when he got home in the evening. I always got there before he did because of the kids. To tell the truth, I kind of liked having this little part of my life to myself.

"I don't need to tell anybody anything," I said.

Once I got used to the routine, the weeks rolled by quickly. Then Gen and Kevin surprised me by leaving for the whole month of September. Said they needed a vacation and went to California, just like that. I'm not sure they'd even really planned it. They kept paying me, even though I only had to come in to water the plants and feed Pat. One day, I found a note pinned to the door, and when Kevin called me, as he did once a week, he told me to just leave it with the mail. I didn't know then, but it was clear that at least one person had found their way to the house. When they got back, they put a motorized gate at the bottom of that long driveway, and later they put a sign down there—one of those fancy brass things that said, "The Jones Family."

Life was good in a lot of ways. In the beginning, Rusty didn't mind that I was working, as long as I was home when he got there.

The kids were fine, too. My ma took to watching Scooter like it was her life's fulfillment, which was good for both of them, since she'd been in a hard place after my daddy left again.

The funny thing about Rusty (not funny in a ha-ha kind of way) is that he can complain a lot about something, but when it goes away, he's all over it like head lice on a first grader. He used to complain that I talked too much, and I think he never understood what it was like to be home with little children all day. You just store up all kinds of things to say to the first grown-up to walk in the door. Anyway, because of Gen and Kevin, I had to be real careful, because sometimes when I get going, I just can't seem to stop. I was worrying all the time about spilling the beans. I still had plenty to say to him when he got home, that's a fact. I recounted everything that happened to the kids at school (since they'd tell me on the way home). I always talked about Ma and her day with Scooter, or her latest complaint about Daddy and his new girlfriend, Francie.

After a while, Rusty started quizzing me about work. I'd tell him about all the housework I did. He'd want to know who came to stay, so I just used my imagination and a little truth about the people who came for healings. He knew that I worked for a couple named Saunders; Genuine had said that would be okay since people don't generally know so much about Kevin. I told Rusty that her name was Genevieve since that was true, too. But Rusty's a smart guy, and maybe he could tell I was holding something back, but he couldn't catch me at it. So he started giving me grief over other stuff, like how I folded the laundry and how organized I kept the kitchen, just things that came naturally since I did it all day long.

All of a sudden, he didn't like the way I put his socks in the drawer. He was a mess of complaints. He even complained about my hair, how he didn't like that I was keeping it up and braided.

"Are you trying to look like some damned hippie?" he asked.

He did like that I'd lost some weight, but I think it made him suspicious, too. One night when we were getting ready for bed, I could tell he was in a foul mood while he was watching me undress.

"Who took the air out of you, Arliss? Who've you been seeing?"

Here's the thing about Rusty. I would have married him even if it hadn't been for Georgie coming along so early. He can be real funny, and he's smart in his own kind of way, but he has these moods. I think it's because he's overwhelmed with the responsibility of this family of ours. When he was in a mood, all I wanted to do was go back to work.

"Like I'd have time to see anyone, and you know it. I'm either at work or here with you and the kids. Besides," I told him, "I don't want to see anybody." Then I made it up to him.

Once when we were out for a movie, Rusty asked me where the B&B was, and there was no way I could say no, so I showed him where the driveway was. I didn't know what he'd think, and I knew that someday I was going to have to tell him the whole thing, but I was always hoping it wouldn't be this day, whatever day it was.

"It's kind of a weird place for a B&B, out of the way like this," he'd said. It was before the sign got installed.

"Most of their guests are from referrals," I told him. And that was true. "Mr. Saunders also does some kind of Internet work, too," I said.

Genuine had told me that Kevin spent a lot of time trying to hide traces of her on the Internet. I know because I went online at the library and looked. We only have one computer at home, and I didn't want Rusty to see what I'd been looking at. One site talked about Genuine when she was younger and said that she no longer healed people. Most of the other stuff was just wrong—wrong picture, wrong description. Some place said she was a charlatan that the Catholics had used to defraud people of their money. It was shameful, but Genuine said that was all Kevin's work. I asked her how people found her, and she said it was mostly word-of-mouth and referrals. And even those people had to go through a lot to find her. I didn't ask what that meant.

After I showed him where the house was, Rusty only asked me occasional questions about work, and the kids were keeping us so busy that it was easy to keep work at work. Being with Kevin and Gen was like having another family, a secret family. Sometimes we'd talk about this or that famous person who would come, how they looked different from the movies or whatever, if it happened that I'd caught a glimpse. Kevin liked me to stay out of the way. But Genuine had this way of keeping it all kind of normal. I don't know how else to explain it. I'd been careful not to ask more questions, and I think the three of us just got comfortable with the arrangement. When I went home, I was so busy with the kids and Rusty, I just didn't think about it much. It was like I was living two lives.

A couple of weeks ago, we had Ma and her old school friend Brenda, who was visiting from Tennessee, for supper one night. It's been a hot summer, and we had a barbecue while the kids were playing in the aboveground pool we put in the backyard. Brenda didn't bring her third husband, Arthur, who used to sell cars before he became some kind of minister. We don't see them much; they've lived in so many different places. Anyway, I about choked on my corn when Brenda started talking about how she'd heard there was a devil-worshipping woman healer near here and how Arthur was going to call on some of the preachers in the area to see about getting the word out to forbid their congregations to have anything to do with her. My mother says that Brenda reinvents herself with every husband.

I started cramming food in my mouth and taking seconds of everything because I knew I just needed to keep my mouth shut.

"Whoa, Arliss. Little hungry there?" Rusty sounded a bit alarmed. I think he was getting used to the new, skinnier me.

"I looked her up on the Internet. There's not a whole lot about her, but some people say she cured them of cancer. She must be taking part of their souls for that," Brenda said. She has a face that looks smug even in her sleep.

It's not that I haven't been all over this in my mind. Rusty's parents weren't so religious, but my brother and I grew up going to Sunday school, at least until my parents split up when I was fifteen. Ma was so embarrassed that she didn't go to church for years after the first time Daddy left her, especially since he left her for one of her church friends, who kept going to church. Anyway, I did think a lot about Genuine's healing power and where it came from. I just can't see that it comes from a bad place.

"What's her name?" Rusty asked.

"Genuine Eriksson. Can you believe that? Who would name a child that?" Brenda said.

She didn't have any kids of her own, even though she had all kinds of opinions about how to raise them.

"Oh, I heard of her," Rusty said. Once again I shoved in some food. I'd already chewed half the inside of my mouth. "Yeah, a long time ago, I saw her on some TV show. She'd supposedly healed some movie star, and I think she went on TV to talk about it. Or maybe the movie star talked about it, and they interviewed Genuine. She lives here now?"

When I heard Rusty say her name, I felt like all of that food I was eating was going to come right back up. I put my fork down.

Brenda said, "Well, no one knows exactly where, but apparently some friend of a relative to Hazel Bell had a friend who took their child to her."

"Who's Hazel Bell?" Ma asked. She was just starting to get interested in what Brenda was saying. Before this she'd been feeding ice cream to Scooter, who was sitting in her lap.

Georgie and Brandy were scooping buckets of water out of the pool and dumping them on each other's heads.

"She's an elderly member of our congregation. Arthur's looking into it."

"Looking into what?" Rusty said.

"Looking into finding out exactly where she lives." Then Brenda looked around the table as if she were some college professor who just realized her students were kindergarteners. "Arthur says he has to find her so he can make her stop."

"Stop what?" Ma asked.

"Stop healing people and taking their souls," Brenda said.

"How do you know that's what she does?" I couldn't help myself. I just had to say it. Brenda would believe anything her fool husband told her.

"How do you know she can even really heal people? It's probably just some celebrity trick," Rusty said.

Brenda glared at Rusty and shook her head at me. Ma picked up Scooter, took him over to the pool, and dangled his feet in. The other kids came over and splashed her and Scooter. Thankfully there was enough commotion that I could just get up and start clearing the dishes. Rusty seemed to lose interest in the whole conversation and went inside and turned on the NASCAR race. Brenda stood up and told Ma that she thought they should leave, as she wanted to drive back home before it was too late, so they left, and the conversation was over.

For a week, I could barely sleep. I didn't tell Kevin or Genuine about it either. I don't know why, but I couldn't. Maybe I was embarrassed to tell them I even knew someone like Brenda—or that she was my ma's friend. I waited every day for Rusty to bring it up. He never did. But I knew that I was going to have to tell him.

Then Rusty had his accident. I don't know how it happened, but he'd been working weekends on his friend Donny's GTO. Donny likes to do some street racing, and he and his car had been at our house all weekend. All I know is, Rusty was under the hood, and Donny was in the car when it happened. It was a flash fire, and I know that Rusty isn't dumb enough to prime the carburetor with gasoline, but I could hear the whoosh from the kitchen and Rusty screaming. I didn't have time to think; I just yelled at Donny to get my mother to come take care of the kids and got Rusty in the car and drove him right to Genuine's. I could barely look at Rusty's face, it was so awful. His hair was singed almost down to the scalp. One arm was burned, too, and he was trying not to yell but not having much luck at it. The turnoff to Gen's is on the way to the hospital, so at first Rusty didn't notice, but when I had to stop to put in the key code to get the gate open, he just went crazy. I kept telling him it would be all right—to trust me. All I could think of was that I hoped he wasn't in that twenty percent of Gen's. I didn't even consider what it would mean for her or for my job. I just had to get Rusty some help.

A beeper goes off in the house when the gate is opened, so I knew they'd be watching for whoever was coming up the drive, although I never knew anyone but me to have the code. Clients and deliveries have to be buzzed in from the house. Halfway up the drive, I nearly panicked when I started to think they might not even be home. They could be out riding their bikes.

I didn't have to worry. Kevin was in the driveway waiting to see who it was. When he saw my car and saw that I wasn't alone, there were a few expressions that danced across his face, and they mostly had to do with frowning. Then he looked closer and rushed to open Rusty's door and ran to call Genuine.

"It's going to be all right, Rusty. She can fix you." I kept saying this over and over as I helped him get out of the car.

"Who can fix me? What are you talking about?" It was a good thing he was in so much distress, because even as he said this, Kevin was leading him into the house and into the living room. Genuine came running down the stairs, her hair flying all over as if she'd just got dressed. I'd never seen her without the braids.

She didn't have to ask anything. I think she could tell right away, although I did say, "This is my husband, Rusty. He was in . . ."

She just reached for Rusty's good arm and took his hand. "How do you do, Rusty? I'm Genuine."

I went and called my mother to be sure that she had the kids. I also told her that we'd overreacted and that the flash didn't really burn anything but Rusty's hair. She seemed okay with that and said she'd tell Donny.

Rusty, once Gen was done with him, just kept glancing around, down at his arm, then around again like a lost pound puppy looking for his mother. He looked at me, too, but kind of out of the side of his eyes. He didn't say much, but he did say, "Thank you," to Genuine about a dozen times.

I talked all the way home in the car, and he didn't say a word. I couldn't tell if he was mad or just in shock. I told him all the reasons why I hadn't said anything about Genuine, about the agreement I'd signed, and how getting the job had depended on that. I told him how Kevin was always trying to protect Genuine from the public, so the secrecy made sense. I told him about how I thought Genuine had healed my asthma, too. He didn't say one word.

When we got home, Ma was all over him with sweet tea and worry. She's always been partial to Rusty, and he has always liked her attention. But he didn't say much to her either, just went into the bedroom and shut the door. Ma went in later and offered him supper, but he said no.

Part of me felt like a stranger in my own house. Now that Rusty knew about Kevin and Genuine, I felt like my world had changed. There was no separating my life there and my life here anymore. It was all mixed up together, and I didn't know how to feel about that. I also knew I'd have to tell Genuine about Brenda and her ilk who were searching for her.

When I went to bed, Rusty looked like he was sleeping, so I didn't say anything. I just got ready as quietly as I could and slid under the covers next to him. He was rolled away from me. I turned the light out. Then real softly, he said, "Don't ever lie to me again."

"Okay," I said.

"Arliss?" he said.

"Yes?"

"Are you going to lose your job now?"

"No, I don't think so."

"Good."

Miscalculation

September 2009

She realized as she came down the hill toward the intersection that she should have taken the other way home, her B route. During rush hour, the intersection could get backed up twenty cars deep, but you never knew how heavy the traffic would be until you got around the curve. The road ended at a stoplight, arrows on the ground clearly defining the options: left lane to go straight, right lane to go straight or right. Every day she chose the left lane. Once you got the green, the right lane quickly disappeared as the road channeled to single lanes coming and going over the San Dieguito Lagoon bridge. Most drivers choosing the right lane were doing it to turn, but inevitably a car next to her would elect to go straight, and there would be a moment of decision as to who got to go first.

It was a dance, really; someone had to take the lead. She always deferred to the driver on the right because he (it was always a he) had invested in the odds that he would get there (wherever there was) before all of those saps waiting in line on the left. Not that she wasn't ever in a hurry. She just didn't think those few extra moments made that much difference. What were a few moments in a life? Today, she was first in line at the light. A long line of cars had come and gone from the right lane, turning off to the other direction. Then a car pulled up next to her and stopped. A quick glance told her all she needed to know.

It was a middle-aged man in a Mercedes convertible. He would surely edge her out when the light changed, passing her from the right as they quickly approached the narrow bridge. That the whole lagoon area had been restored to a marshy primitive habitat was a wonderful thing. That a section of this harried commuter access had been widened was a good thing. The funnel-clogging effect of the single lane bridge was just weird. She'd never bothered to investigate the reason. By the time she got through that patch of traffic, it would leave her awareness like a fly escaping a car window on a highway.

As she sat waiting for the light to turn, she glanced again at the man in the Mercedes—dyed hair, neat white shirt and tie. She did this surreptitious survey in less than five seconds. She definitely didn't want him to see her looking. She took her foot off the brake and let her car move forward just a bit. She could feel that the Merc Man was now looking at her. She was driving a twelve-year-old minivan. A family car. A woman's car. An older woman driver. Not that she was so much older than this man.

This was a ninety-second light, necessary to manage the three-way traffic. There were a lot of seconds left. The Mercedes pulled forward a bit. She wasn't surprised; she was expecting it. She was not in a race with this man. She didn't care enough. She had a small but undeniable amount of scorn for people like this, though she didn't like to admit it. She strived to be above contempt and derision, but old ways of thinking could creep in unannounced. There really was a certain loser quality to a middle-aged man with dyed hair driving a convertible Mercedes, aiming to gain a five-minute advantage on his drive home. That was approximately how long he would have had to wait in the left lane with everyone else if he hadn't used this lane to steal up beside her.

Sometimes she liked to wonder about people's lives. What did this man do for a living? What was his wife (or in this case, most assuredly his girlfriend) like? What did he do with his kids on their visitation weekends? She sighed. She was being unkind. He inched forward again. The light was not ready to change: no yellow in the other direction.

Although it had been a long day, she wasn't in a hurry. No one was waiting. Kids grown. Husband gone. Boyfriend gone. Dog recently dead. She missed him a lot, the dog, that is. There were good things, too. A recent promotion. Girlfriends. Time to read. A mortgage nearly paid off. Her savings intact (including money she'd been setting aside to get a newer vehicle). She let her car slide about a foot forward. She didn't look to her right. She kept her eyes steadily on the light.

Yellow, green, foot to the floor. She couldn't say why. She couldn't even pinpoint the moment her foot slid off the brake and onto the gas. Whatever primitive impulse came from her brain to her ankle to press downward on the pedal seemed to bypass her higher cognitive functions. The acceleration was short; her foot flexed off the gas, eased back onto the brake, and she was back in the moment, casually glancing in her review mirror. Merc Man was smirking. Interesting. That's what she did every time someone beat her out in traffic. There was something about his smirk. It was personal. Disdain, with an intimacy about it. A connection. She could also tell he got it, got who he was. Who he was trying to be? Or perhaps he thought he knew who she was, who she was trying to be.

She glanced back again. Then in her periphery, on this single no-bike-lane road, were two cyclists. She had to swerve quickly, then over-adjust in the other direction since traffic was coming thickly. Cars veared, she braked, and one cyclist slid onto the rough and narrow gravel shoulder. The other fell on top of the first in no time—yellow and black tangled up in a honeycomb of appendages and spinning spokes. And then, the bump from behind, in a kind of screeching, slow-motion dream sequence. All now at a halt. Horns blowing and perhaps some shouting as cars further behind saw their escape home laid to waste, at least for some time.

She was not hurt. Her airbag had not deployed. But something was pulling her under, deep down into some pit of dark remorse, and she couldn't catch her breath. It must be like this to drown, she thought. Someone opened her door, and an arm reached in and unbuckled her seat belt. The same arm pulled her out of the car and led her by the elbow to the cyclists on the ground. She saw a helmet with long black braids leaning over another helmeted cyclist—a man sitting on the ground, one eye peering through an empty frame, the other covered in a praying mantis lens. One of his legs was bent up at the knee, the other leg outstretched, red and tarred with gravel and blood. A Gash. She felt sick.

The helmet with braids turned, and she wondered why she had thought of this woman as a disembodied head. She was looked at and dismissed as the woman returned to caring for the man.

"I'm so sorry. I didn't see you." No response. "Are you okay?" she asked the man. "Should I call an ambulance?"

The man looked at his companion, and she could see the braided helmet swivel back and forth.

"No, I'll be fine."

"No, really, I think I should call someone," she said. She was starting to get her bearings.

She felt, only now realizing, a hand on her elbow. Then the hand was gone as the Merc Man picked up the bicycles and fiddled with them: setting them upright, checking the wheels, and inspecting the chains.

"I think your bikes are okay," he said to the couple on the ground.

"Thanks." The helmet tilted up. The face was pointed in Merc Man's direction, away from her.

She realized that traffic had begun to flow around them, finding the long stretch of empty lane in front of her car. The oncoming traffic slowed and acquiesced to the alteration like two opposing lines of ants marching around an insurmountable obstacle.

All of this in five minutes, she thought. Five life-changing minutes.

Merc Man was talking to the couple again. He was handing them his card. The woman tried to give it back, but the man on the ground took it and tucked it into his pocket. He stood, and she could see the dirt and gravel on his leg but could no longer see blood. Perhaps she'd been wrong about the gash. The woman must have cleaned it off with something.

Then there was a hand with a card in front of her. She looked at the white-shirted arm and then up to the face. She'd been wrong; the hair wasn't dyed. Plenty of gray around the edges, and lines, too. A small paunch at the waist. She looked down at the card: Allen and Allen, Attorneys at Law. David Allen. Shit. And then, shit. Shit.

She exhaled, inhaled, and looked up at his face. There was that smirk, but the eyes were smiling. The smirk was really a crooked smile, some asymmetry, imperfection, in his face. She didn't think there was condescension.

"Your car is damaged," he said. "But not very much."

"So is yours," she said.

They stood near the back of her car and the front of his where their fenders met at the juncture. She watched as the cyclists mounted their bikes as if nothing had happened. Something tugged at her mind, but the man was talking.

"Not much. And it's not mine," he said. "It's my father's. I was taking it in for repairs."

He was holding her by the elbow again, this time with his left hand, his right softly on the small of her back—a simple caress of courtesy. He looked her over from head to toe.

"Okay," she said. "I should give you my information, too."

She started to reach into the car for her purse, but he was still holding her by the elbow. "I think the cars will survive," he said, and then, "Call me," as he let her go.

She drove slowly over the bridge, past the empty soccer fields, all the way to the signal. The cyclists were nowhere to be seen.

The Beginning and the End

July 2012

It was a year of petty grievances and small apologies. After I healed that boy in California, we had to regroup a bit because Kevin was right. Healing someone in the middle of the road (without taking our normal non-disclosure precautions) would surely get noticed. I didn't really have a choice; he was an eight-year-old child, after all. The media got wind, and we had to lay low. Very low. We couldn't risk a maelstrom. For two months, we didn't take calls or answer messages, and I never left the house. We put a sold sign down at the driveway entrance, let fake mail pile up in the mailbox that we never used (we always used a PO Box), and eventually put up a new sign that said, "Olmstead Home." It was mostly Kevin's idea, this hunkering down, and it also had the deepest impact on him. But it was too late to start over, because we were over, although neither of us would say it.

It started over the coffee we didn't have when five people were scheduled to show up for healings. Life had returned to some normalcy, and Kevin managed the appointments as he always had, although he was cagier about who got to see me. Arliss was on vacation; it was summer, and her kids were out of school. Lately, Kevin had developed some irrational tick of annoyance when she was around, so I'd told her to take the whole month of July off. At first she wouldn't have it.

I think she didn't want to be home all day with the kids, but I found her a place at the beach and paid for it, though I didn't tell Kevin that part. I thought being alone in the house might soothe the peevish tension that lived under the surface of our skins, like static electricity prickling and sparking in the dryness between us.

"There's no coffee," Kevin said. He didn't say, "Again," but it was a phantom, floating there in the room.

Grocery shopping was Arliss's purview, and Kevin's if she wasn't around. So even though it wasn't my fault, I said, "I'm so sorry." There would be no time for Kevin to make the twenty-minute run to town, and I was sorry. The visitors would be fine with tea or whatever we had on hand, but Kevin liked his coffee.

"You shouldn't have given Arliss the whole month off," Kevin said.

"I thought we'd enjoy the time to ourselves." As I said this, I realized my mistake.

"Time to ourselves was what we used to have in California. Time to ourselves doesn't involve strangers showing up all week for healings. It's not days of recuperating from healing someone who is probably going to go home and continue smoking and drinking and beating his wife. Time to ourselves is life, Gen. Real life."

It's true that I can occasionally be incapacitated after a difficult healing, but that's rare. It happened more when I was a child and couldn't control the energy. I heard once that baby rattlesnakes give the worst bite because they don't have the ability to conserve their venom. That may sound like an inverse analogy, but it's how I understand myself.

It's also true that I've healed people who might not consider themselves responsible for their own health. It's not always possible for me to know these things. Maybe it's not right for me to know, though Kevin thinks I could at least give the ones with the obvious bad habits a little talking to.

Lately Kevin's been sharing a lot of his ideas, but these were points we'd been taking turns with for years. At times, these were my concerns; now they were his. We are nothing if not our shared history, and history cannot be escaped, only misremembered.

"Kevin, you are exaggerating."

"It's a choice, Gen," Kevin said. "You can choose how to live your life. And it's not just your life."

We'd been standing in the kitchen, each separately staring at the coffee maker and the empty canister next to it. We'd inherited a set of green stoneware canisters from the previous owners. I wouldn't have bought them myself, but I'd grown fond of them and their simple hominess. Now they were all empty.

Kevin looked up at me, and there were two things going on. One, he was giving me his full consideration, a look that I know well. It has a kind of forbearance—and love, too. He has been a patient man in some ways. But I could also see that he was looking at something else, or for something else, like what was past me on the other side.

"Our whole life is an exaggeration," he said. His voice was soft with regret.

He turned, and I followed him to the living room, happy to leave the hanging thoughts behind. The living room was ready for our visitors: clean and vacuumed, tables dusted. However, the pictures were still out—pictures of our parents, siblings, and us together, smiling. Pieces of our life, family life, of a sort. We always put these away to preserve our privacy, so I collected and stacked them in the cabinet and shut the door. Kevin sat at the desk going over our list for the day. He handled all of this. I would be upstairs by the time the doorbell rang, since we would have to buzz people in the gate down the long driveway. It was our routine. An old routine.

I would have married Kevin at nineteen, or twenty, or twenty-one. But I'd made a deal with my dad that if I left home with Kevin, I wouldn't get married until I finished college. By the time that happened, we were in the midst of other things and, well, we lost some momentum.

I've loved Kevin in all the ways that I can. In the beginning, I adored him. Aside from the physical attraction, he was so helpful, and the simple truth of my being alive mattered so much to him. With a gift like mine, that's rare. People have so much to gain from me. It has an isolating effect.

Loving him now is different. I've grown up; he's grown older, though his age is not a problem for me. I like the way his curls are starting to fleck out in gray around the edges of his face. There is a spot on the side of his neck that compels me to touch, to lay my hand and feel the thrill of his pulse. And there is a spot on my lower back where his touch can send me swooning still. In all things sexual, we are well-matched. He is a good man. But he cannot save me from myself nor from all the little things he thinks I need saving from, and I cannot make the sacrifice he needs. I cannot choose between him and who I am. I cannot choose to stop healing.

I went up behind him while he sat there at his desk and put my hand on that spot. The heel of my hand on the back of his neck, fingers feeling the pulse of his carotid, the force of blood pumping from his heart: left ventricle to aortic arch to my hand. I put my head forward to rest my chin on his head at the same moment he was shrugging me away. There was no violence intended on his part, but we were both injured in our own ways, his head meeting my chin, his eyes meeting mine as he stood and turned. There was more pain in the look, of course, than in my chin or his head. These small acts, this small moment, loomed as large as our beginning. I went upstairs to wait, feeling the blood pounding in my chin.

$$\diamond\!\!-\!\!\diamond\!\!-\!\!\diamond$$

I like the moments of sitting and waiting for the clients to come. There is a thrill in the anticipation, for the experience, for the question of whether it will work, for the things that I might learn, and for the ways in which my ability can surprise me. It was like this, waiting for Kevin to come back to me all those years ago, after his surgery.

"Even though the doctor said there was no cancer, I still didn't believe you'd healed me."

"Really?" I'd said. "How do you think you got over the cancer?"

"I thought the doctors had made a mistake. That I'd never had cancer."

"So why did you come back?"

I'd told him he needed to come back to Des Moines for more healing. I also lied and told him I was nearly twenty. I was just shy of nineteen and full of heady passion and desire for a different life. I didn't know if he'd fall for me, but I hoped for it, thought about it, dreamt about it, and planned for it. I was young. I had the day-dreams of the young.

He has a slight dimple in his left cheek when he grins a certain way. I call it his ironic dimple. He shrugged.

"Why not? How could I resist flinging myself off into something so kooky and unbelievable?" And then he got serious and said, "All of a sudden, what I'd come to expect for my future—financial success, European trips, Cynthia's vision of a perfectly ordained family life—didn't seem so appealing. I had to come back."

I lied to my parents, too, and said there was some leftover cancer I thought I could cure. I think most adolescents have this careless relationship with the truth. It was a few weeks before my birthday and right before my trip to Rome. My mother was in a flurry of anxious preparation and distracted enough to leave me on my own with Kevin. I told Kevin I'd need to see him for several days in a row. My parents knew all about how healing worked, so deep down, I'm pretty sure they knew something was up. My dad invited Kevin to dinner two nights in a row, talking to him man-to-man about sports teams and the stock market as if he were a friend his age, trying to accentuate the gap in our ages. I didn't care.

I told Kevin he needed to come back again in August after my trip. He knew then that I was lying about needing to cure him more, but by then he was in love with me, too.

◇

I went away to school in September, living in the dorms. My parents had arranged for me to have a private room. They felt it would be safer and easier to keep my gift a secret. I should stop saying "gift." I should just say "ability."

Kevin came to visit me three or four times. I didn't tell my parents. We had long philosophical discussions. Kevin, post-cancer, was considering God and the general meaning of life. I—post-Catholic school, post-disappointing visit to the pope, and newly out of my parents' nest—was more interested in exploring the corporeal aspects of life. It wasn't hard to persuade him.

Cynthia also showed up once that fall. I was walking from one class to another, English to history or history to anatomy and physiology (a course I took to help identify the experiences I had during healing). I saw this very chic woman walking toward me, looking not at all like a student, nor in the least like a professor, staring directly at me as if she knew me.

"You're her, aren't you?" she said as she approached.

I had not healed anyone since I'd come to campus, and I had not talked to anyone about it either. I promised my parents and Kevin, because all anyone wanted for me was to enjoy my college experience. I had not expected my freedom to be so proscribed, but for the moment, I was abiding by their expectations.

Perhaps she knew someone I'd healed at St. Timothy's. Perhaps someone told her what I looked like and where I attended school. It seemed so unlikely, although there was Father Hanson, who I could very well imagine seeking retribution for the fact that I didn't take the full scholarship he'd procured for me to Rosemont College.

"I'm who?" I asked.

"You're the healer, Genevieve Eriksson. You healed my fiancé, Kevin."

"I don't think he's your fiancé anymore." I didn't know whether Kevin had misled me, but I wasn't going to start by giving her the advantage.

She narrowed her eyes and looked me over. I thought this was something she shouldn't do—her eyes were already a hair too close to center. That was unkind, of course, but I was young. She took her time in quiet appraisal. I wore jeans and a baggy sweatshirt, and my hair hung down my back in a day-old braid. This was my normal weekday wardrobe. It was all around me in those days, this sloppy college look, except for the sorority girls. I wasn't looking to attract attention, nor was I interested in attracting boys. I was in love with a full-grown man.

"You're taking advantage of him, his condition," she said. She was pretty, despite the eyes, in a perfectly groomed kind of way: a jacket of fine soft wool with matching slacks, her brown hair in place to a fault.

"He has no condition," I countered.

"I sent him to you. You wouldn't have cured him if it weren't for me."

I should have felt something—sympathy, guilt, insecurity because she referred to Kevin as her fiancé. None of that came to me.

"I love him," I said.

"You're too young to know what love is. You don't know Kevin, and you don't know what he needs."

A cold wind kicked up, anticipating what the dusky clouds over-head were bringing. Her hair started to bob around her face a bit. I put my book bag down and wound my braid up on my head so I could put my hood up.

I swung the bag over my shoulder and said, "I have to get to class." I walked past her slowly so that she might think I was unperturbed.

I could hear her let out a breath with a little grunt. She followed me, her heels clicking along the sidewalk. She walked abreast of me, then advanced and turned in front so that I had to stop.

"Please," she said. "We were going to get married." She hadn't lost an ounce of her chic-ness. I wondered if this was her courtroom approach, a final feminine plea to the jury.

My ability is limited to physical ailments. I can't heal broken hearts, but the energy that flows through me is a powerful thing when it comes.

"Cynthia," I said and held out my hand.

"You know my name?" Her face fell slightly. I could see her contemplating what she probably hadn't considered, that Kevin had told me about her, which she must have known but hadn't yet faced.

Cynthia looked at my hand and deliberated for a moment. Then she said, "No, I don't think so." She turned and walked away.

I stood for a moment with my hand still outstretched. I'm not sure what I had planned to do. I think I had wanted to give her a taste of my strength.

Kevin was appalled when he heard, but Cynthia left him alone after that. I moved off campus in January into an apartment with Kevin. There was a gale over that at home, but eventually we all reached a middle ground. Over the years, my parents have come to treat Kevin like my spouse and otherwise stay out of whatever is going on with us.

—◇—

I sat in the blue room, waiting for the first appointment. I was thinking that I might end up with a bruise on my chin. Kevin would feel bad about that. The house had several bedrooms, and I used two of them for healing. We called the other one the yellow room. They were decorated as they were when we bought the house several years ago—southern country-style B&B. The generic décor suited our purpose; people were comfortable with it, and putting any kind of personal stamp on it would only lift the veil of our private life a little more. We'd thought all of these things through over the years. Everybody I heal wants to be my friend, Kevin's friend. We have to keep such a strict circle around ourselves. I needed to release Kevin from that, change the shape of our lives without changing who I am. I needed to be released, too, from his watchful, careful, expectant love.

My cell phone rang from a distance. I wondered if Arliss was calling, or one of my brothers. Kevin would answer it and tell them about our schedule for the day. It was nice to have someone with whom we could share the ordinary moments of our unordinary life. A few minutes later, Kevin knocked and opened the door. I got up, thinking I would be greeting our first client of the day. He was alone.

He stood in the doorway looking serious, my cell phone in his hand.

"I can't," I said. "I can't marry you." I hadn't planned to say it and was surprised that I had.

I didn't understand the pity in his look. I don't know what I'd been expecting, but it wasn't that. Then he handed me the phone and said, "It's your mother." As I took the phone, the gate buzzer sounded, and Kevin pulled the door shut. Click.

My brother Lars had been in an accident, a serious one, outside of Des Moines while visiting my parents. It took me some moments before I could make the shift from here to there, to imagine what it meant: body flying end over end in one direction as the motorcycle slid in the other, lightning sparks of metal to macadam, and corn stalks bowing in the wind, shivering at such a sight. Then I was there in the moment of shock, and all the previous days and months of torpid thoughts of existence and meaning shuttled to the background.

When I looked up, Kevin was there, waiting. I hadn't heard him return. He said, "I'll call the airlines." And then, "I'll tell the client to go, and cancel the others."

"No," I said, "send this one up. He's already here." I looked at him, wondering what to say next.

"I'll pack," he said. Of course he would. Kevin the Keeper.

The knock on the door was Kevin's soft knock. I realized I could recognize his knock anywhere. When I opened the door, Kevin, who stood behind the client, was watching me with worry and concern. Lars's accident had preempted his anger over my announcement. He was back to protecting me. I couldn't bear it. I took the client by the arm and drew him into the room and shut the door with a quickness that I regretted. I was coming undone.

The client was near my age, a man of burly build and sallow, jaundiced skin. His hair was thick-cut and bristly, standing up short in military salute. He reminded me of Danny Fowler, or how Danny Fowler might have looked at this age if he hadn't died in a farm accident at the age of twenty-six. I had always felt I owed Danny Fowler something for being the first to recognize my abilities, bully though he was. This man's name was Larry. He wasn't Danny Fowler, but he was very sick.

"Did I come at a bad time?" He had a soft, unexpectedly gentle voice. Fear of death can do that, upend who you are—or were. Particularly in men.

"It is a bad time for us, I'm sorry. But it won't interfere with the healing."

I was already holding his hand and could feel the energy flowing, with its rising heat and the lightness that I allowed myself to succumb to. Kevin has every right to be jealous of this. I am an island he can't swim to.

By the time I was done with Larry, Kevin had packed our bags, cancelled the clients for the next few days, arranged our airfare, and called Arliss to tell her what happened. Before we left the house, I had my mother put the phone up to Lars's ear and tried to send some healing to him, but it's always tricky. I wasn't getting any response—no heat, no feeling of connection. He was groggily conscious.

"Hey, Sparky," I said. "I'm on my way; you'll be okay." I don't have foresight, and I'm not omniscient, but I am a sister, and I said what I had to believe.

◇

It took us all day to get to Lars in Des Moines: two hours to the airport in Charlotte, a layover in Chicago. Kevin and I didn't speak much on the way.

Lars, the youngest in our family, came into the world gregarious, sweet, smart, and funny. I hand it to my parents for making our childhood as normal as possible, despite the church, and despite me. I think raising Andrew and Lars turned out to be a relief for my parents, particularly after I left. Things could settle down, and typical family life could take over. Lars got engaged to Stephanie this year, the first family wedding looming on the horizon in the fall.

By the time we got to the hospital, the news was grim and had been, actually, since we landed in Chicago. My dad met us in the lobby, looking bleak and hopeful at the same time.

"I'm so glad you're here, so glad we have you," he said while holding me tight to his chest.

I've done healings in hospitals, of course, but not in a while. I wasn't prepared to see Lars this way—tubes and everything, his red hair cropped around the bandages, the squeak at the end of each exhalation of the respirator. Andrew hadn't made it in yet from Seattle but was on his way. I didn't have to look at anyone to know that now I, not Lars, was the center of attention and expectation. I held Lars's limp hand, waiting, for everyone's sake, for something I wasn't sure would happen.

As a baby and toddler, Lars had eyes that were wide in a state of constant amused amazement, as if the world was a wonder to him. He grew to be a great mimic and loved to entertain us with impersonations of not only our parents, but also of Andrew and me, and eventually Kevin. He would mock me the hardest, and I would laugh the loudest. We talked every week. I'd been the first he'd told about Stephanie, and he and I had sat for hours, cell phones to our ears, browsing the Internet for her engagement ring. The love was unbreakable.

It's not working. I couldn't say it aloud, but everyone knew.

Stephanie was on the other side of the bed, my parents by Lars's feet. Kevin was standing by the doorway.

"You can keep trying, right?" Stephanie said. I'd only met her once, and I'm sure she knew all about me, but perhaps not the part about my failures.

"You're probably just tired from your trip," my mother said. She knew better. "Perhaps we should all leave you alone here with Lars."

"Okay, maybe that will help." Against all experience, I wanted to believe it. I had to believe it.

I stayed with him all night trying to conjure up some heat, some energy. I have worried about some clients who didn't get healed, particularly a child or young mother. I have been surprised over the years by how quickly a healing might go for some people I knew—just by the set of their mouth or the viciousness in their eyes—I would never befriend and would avoid if I ever saw them again. I came alone to this, without a guidebook or rules. It either works or it doesn't.

I put the guardrail down so I could lay my head next to Lars's.

"Wake up, Sparky," I whispered. "Please."

I thought of the pictures my father took when we were young, the three of us, heads together: blond, black, and red. We were our own flag of the small country of Eriksson.

I closed my eyes, and sleep lurked like a ghost amid the sound effects. Whoosh. Whoosh. Squeak. Whoosh. Anything, just a little, if I could get it flowing, then perhaps the heat would build. Whoosh. Whoosh. Squeak. After a while, Stephanie came back and sat across from me. My parents were in and out all night. The nurses alternately asked us to leave and left us alone.

No one seemed to know who I was, and at that moment, I doubted, too, that I'd ever healed anyone. My entire life had been a dream that I was now waking up from, like an amnesiac without a past.

In the morning, the doctors came and drew my parents out of the room, then they came for Stephanie and me. I wouldn't go. I didn't want to talk about it. I knew, but I didn't want to hear. They waited until Andrew came, and I kept trying, knowing it wouldn't work.

At 11:54 a.m., Lars, my brother, was disconnected from his life-support machine and died.

The day of the funeral brought hundred-degree temperatures and oppressive humidity. My dad, Andrew, Kevin, and some cousins carried the casket out of the hearse to the gravesite. Kevin had planned ahead and packed a black skirt and white blouse for me and a dark suit for himself. He knew it had been a mistake when he saw that I took notice of this preparation.

Back at the house, the Irish side drank their grief in the open, and the Swedish side held onto theirs behind quiet mouths and faces of strict control. My parents looked confused and out of place among the relatives in this new old house of theirs. When the boys moved away, our parents shook off the remnants of their suburban life and moved closer to town to a lovely old Craftsman-style house. The house is larger than it looks from the street and could house all of us in separate rooms. I knew they were waiting for grandchildren. They were united, finally, in their expectancy of this common family pleasure. They loved Stephanie, lovely Stephanie, who would have had lovely babies with Lars. Stephanie wept quietly, swallowed in the oversized Stickley chair in the corner of the living room. Kevin served drinks, cleaned up, and made himself useful. He talked to Andrew; he left me alone. Everyone left me alone.

—◇—

"Gen, it's too soon to talk about it. You need to grieve. I'll be fine. I'll just go home and wait for you."

I was driving Kevin to the airport. I was glad to be driving so I could keep my eyes forward.

"No. I can't come back. I'm sorry, Kevin."

We had said all of this before, of course, during the week we spent with my parents after the funeral. At the airport, I got out of the car and hugged him. He looked older. It was the first time I noticed the softening around his jaw line, a new line on his forehead. He's fifty. I've wasted so much of his time.

I started back toward the car and turned. He was already wheeling his suitcase away, his back to me.

"Kevin." He turned.

"Tell people I'm done. I'm not a healer anymore."

"Then why—?" But I was back in the car before he could finish.

I drove to the hospital where Lars had died. It was a large hospital on the west side of town. I knew it had a chemo suite because I'd looked it up online. I needed to know. I bought some flowers in a vase in the lobby gift shop and made my way up to the outpatient suite. Several people sat chatting, talking to friends or loved ones. Others were by themselves, watching TV on small monitors or looking straight ahead with terror and resignation. I slipped through the door and looked around in expectation. All those who were patients had IVs running either to their arms or to a port in their chests. Nurses came and went, checked IV bags and monitors and chatted cheerfully. One efficient-looking, dark-haired nurse turned to me.

"Can I help you?"

I had thought this through partially. Holding up the flowers, I said, "I'm looking for Mrs. Jones."

She shook her head, "No Mrs. Jones here today."

"I'm sorry," I said. "I must have the wrong day. She's a friend of my mother's, and I thought today was her chemo day." This little lie was all I'd constructed on the way here.

I approached a young woman who looked as if she were trying to dislodge herself from the environment. It's a look I've seen before: anywhere but here.

I put the flowers on the tray next to her and said, "I can't come back until next week, and these will probably spoil. "You may as well have them."

She glanced at me briefly and nodded. The nurse was glancing my way, and the woman was obviously not going to talk. I didn't want to lose my chance, so I reached into my pocket and grabbed the packet of plant food that came with the flowers. I held it out so she'd have to take it from my hand.

"Here's some flower food," I said, and even then I wasn't sure she'd respond. She was sunk in some distant reverie.

Finally, she glanced up and said, "Thanks," as her hand brushed mine. And there it was, the heat and healing, just like always, beginning to flow through me. I shoved my hand back into the pocket of my skirt.

"I hope you enjoy them," I said, then left. When I got outside, the humidity had lifted as it often does just before a storm. The sky was a mass of anger.

Lillian and Fred and Alejandro

2010 - 2015

"Alejandro." She leaned against the doorjamb, her arms folded across her chest. They were honey-colored with a lifetime of sun, though the skin was now wrinkled and aging it's way toward transparency. She never tired of saying his name. They'd been together for over forty years. She knew he would think of it that way, too.

She smiled, looking first at him, then past him toward the edge of the property and beyond to the vanishing point of the winding road.

"Lillian," Alejandro said. It had taken him years to stop calling her señora.

As he stood there, she could smell the spring jasmine that clung to him. Whatever the season, she could tell from the scent of Alejandro.

He held a basket of oranges and roses from her garden. His straw hat, frayed at the edges, was one that he hung on a nail in the barn each evening when he left, replacing it with a cowboy hat that he kept in the back seat of his truck.

For the last few years, Fred played a slow game of golf every Wednesday with Henry, an old friend. They would play nine holes and then have an easy lunch at the club. It was good for Fred to get out without her, away from her watchful eye.

Alejandro had been there the first time Fred had a stroke, although

Lillian hadn't realized what had happened at the time. He'd fallen, passed out briefly, and awakened confused.

"The oranges look perfect," she said. "Come in. Lunch is ready."

Alejandro stepped through the doorway and said, "Perhaps for a little while."

It was what he always said. It was their Wednesday routine. Lillian would make lunch in the morning, usually simple things—sandwiches and soup or a salad—and Alejandro would bring her a basket from the garden around noon. Their speech, the opening lines, here at the door had become a little script, a polite pas de deux of formality.

It had not been easy to persuade him in the beginning. The first few times she had offered to cook for him, he had politely refused.

"Why don't you come in early and have lunch, and then we can talk?" she'd said.

They had often met at her kitchen table to talk about the garden and the orchards. In the beginning, Fred had made some noise about inviting the outside help inside the house, but that was in the past. Fred was sweet now after his strokes. He seemed happy that Alejandro would keep her company while he golfed. Sweet, she thought, of all things.

"Thank you, Lillian," Alejandro had replied, "but Alicia packed my lunch. She would be disappointed if I didn't eat it. And I need to wait by the barn for some deliveries."

On the second try, Lillian insisted that Alejandro bring his lunch into the house and join her. The third time, he made excuses again, so Lillian suggested that he give Alicia a break once a week from making his lunch. Alicia was Alejandro's daughter, who worked full-time and had three children. Lillian was not going to give up. He knew that, too.

So every week, the little formalities they shared at the door were, to her, a kind of foreplay for the sensual thrill she experienced while listening to his voice over lunch and for the garden scent that he brought indoors. She had initially made some attempts to make him

Mexican food. He was always polite about whatever she made, but she'd gotten a call from Alicia telling her, confidentially, that her father would really prefer something simple. Lillian didn't press the matter with Alicia—the nature of her culinary faux pas. She stuck to simpler fare.

Now Alejandro carried the basket to the kitchen and placed his hat on the corner of one of the ladder-back chairs. He went to the powder room and washed up, arriving back at the table with his hair wet and combed back from his face. By the end of their lunch, Lillian knew from experience, the natural wave of his hair would have tugged his gray-flecked tendrils back toward his face. It was a lovely thing to watch.

"We will have to cut the other eucalyptus down," Alejandro said as he pulled out the chair and sat. There were many eucalyptus trees on the property, but Lillian knew which one he referred to. "I can see the fungus," he said. "We'd better cut it down before this one spreads, too."

Alejandro had come north from Mexico with his parents when he was ten, one of six children. His father had worked for Lillian's father. When Lillian and Fred married, Alejandro came to work for them on the ten-acre property that Lillian's parents helped them purchase. It came with a barn and five acres of lemon orchards—one hundred and fifty trees per acre. They planted an additional two acres of oranges and an acre of limes. The produce was handled by a local company who arranged the picking and selling. It had helped with the house payments. Another acre was left to pasture, and the rest was lovely with a combination of native oaks and the area's signature eucalyptus. The orchards—and the vast collection of flowering plants that Lillian, with Alejandro's help, used to landscape around the house—generated the current that ran the hum of her life.

"Whatever you think," she said, setting two plates with sandwiches on the table. Whenever Lillian had lunch with Alejandro, she always sat in Fred's place at the end of the plank table, Alejandro to her left with his arm close to hers. She enjoyed seeing the contrast of his nut-brown arm to her paler amber-colored one. She liked using the casual Mexican pottery plates her daughter had given her one Christmas. She looked forward to Wednesdays.

From the beginning, Fred and Alejandro had maintained an arm's length relationship, knowing the ways they shared Lillian. There were parts of Lillian that Fred could not comprehend. The garden and orchards seemed to answer a longing in her that he could no more understand than he could satisfy. It made him jealous of Alejandro, and he had asked Lillian from time to time if she was in love with Alejandro. Although he could not imagine it, could not compare himself to Alejandro without seeing himself at a considerable advantage, he'd asked anyway. She always said no, of course not.

Briefly, he took to working around the property himself on weekends, giving up golf games so he could show her that he could do this, too. He bought some expensive equipment: a chain saw, clippers, and a mulcher. He was good at lopping things off and cutting things down.

The jealousy worked at him like a beetle digging a burrow, more so because he had no evidence, and couldn't find any. He once accused Alejandro of stealing his chain saw and fired him one day when Lillian was gone with the children. When she came home and found out, she wept so hard he was sure that it was the grief of finding out that Alejandro was a thief. He was mistaken.

"You crazy, insane man!" she'd shouted. "Two weeks before the garden tour? I don't care what he did!"

Fred had forgotten about the garden tour, being their first year to be selected. He should have remembered. He went to where he had hidden the saw, re-placing it in the barn but covering it first under some tarps, telling her he'd found it there.

"It must have been one of the day laborers who moved it. I'm so sorry, Lilly. I'll call Alejandro right away. I'll make it right. I promise."

Alejandro must have known. He never said anything, but for a long time he went back to calling Lillian señora. Fred was never anything but Señor Walsh. In remorse for his subterfuge, Fred helped Alejandro with naturalization.

Over time, Fred tried other tactics: teaching Lillian to play golf, enrolling them in bridge lessons and dancing lessons. She was interested, but only just so. When the children went off to college, he bought her a horse—a beautiful warmblood from Holland—to remind her that he had known her heart in her youth. But she didn't want to turn the barn back into a stable. She didn't want to rob Alejandro of his domain, Fred assumed. He knew he was right about this. She boarded the horse at the riding club and enrolled in lessons, but eventually lost interest, said it took too much time away from her garden club duties, and sold the horse to a friend. She'd been touched by the gesture, but only just so.

◇—◇—◇

For years, Lillian had known that Fred was competing with Alejandro. She denied all his queries and accusations, but she would not, could not, move Alejandro out of their lives. Not for the sake of her marriage. She'd felt, at the time, that her marriage needed to stand on its own, apart from Fred's jealousies. She had wanted Fred to learn that his jealousy had no sway over her, that she could not submit to his unreasonableness just for his sake. Her sake mattered, too. Without that there could be no marriage. No true commitment. After the stroke, she wondered if it had just been faulty wiring all along, because there was no jealousy now. It was why she hadn't worried when she couldn't reach Genuine; she'd felt like there was nothing to cure. By the time Genuine did arrive, Fred was back to playing golf. He had a few more minor events but was on medication to ward off any more. Ischemic attacks—the fire of jealousy starved of oxygen.

Her experience with cancer had given another face to Fred's jealousies. Jealous because, once again, he'd felt left out. Until she was cured. That changed him a bit. He was in awe that she'd made a decision to use a "healer," of all things, and also that it had worked in her favor. Their life took a new shape for a while. She softened, too. She was careful to arrange dates on the weekends. They went to the symphony. They walked the trails on Sundays.

Several years after her illness but before Fred's stroke, he'd come home from work and said, "I'm having a realtor come by tomorrow."

"Whatever for?"

"We should start thinking about moving to a smaller place. We've talked about the cost of watering the orchards. We're barely breaking even. We could get one of those nice casitas on the golf course."

After the cancer, Lillian had resigned her post at the garden club, but she hadn't lost interest in gardening. It had just become more personal, and in ways she couldn't explain, more deeply gratifying. Small mundane activities, such as weeding or deadheading the roses, gave her new, unexpected satisfaction. Fred wouldn't have noticed this, she realized.

"You can move to a casita if you want, Fred. But the only way I'm leaving is in a casket." She felt chilled and remembered the cancer.

"You expect too much," he said.

Lillian wasn't sure what he meant by that but didn't pursue it because she didn't like where it might lead. She walked out to the front porch and surveyed the land. Fred tried to follow, but she held her hand up and said, "Not now," and walked down to the barn. She called for Alejandro.

"Please, come walk the property with me."

Later, she and Fred had a more civilized conversation.

"We can subdivide and sell part of the orchard—most of the limes, I think, but I'd want to be sure we still have each kind of citrus. We'll have to rearrange some of the trees," she said.

"Okay," Fred said. He knew that Lillian had always been passionately opposed to subdividing. She'd hated the loss of rural character, the newness of the homes that were springing up everywhere, the crowded village streets, and the crowded school. He felt gratified that she'd come to a compromise with him.

"If you sell, it's likely the new owners will subdivide," Alejandro had told Lillian on their walk.

They sold the lot with restrictions on building size and height. They couldn't hide the new house from their view, but she and Alejandro designed a screen of trees and shrubs that at least complemented it.

Sitting at her kitchen table with Alejandro, while he carefully refolded the blue-and-white napkin next to his plate, she remembered that they'd had tumultuous times, too.

When she was young and inexperienced, she often insisted on plants over Alejandro's objections. He knew what would flourish and what would not. If the plants failed, she got angry with him. He would fire back in Spanish so quickly that she couldn't understand it all, but she caught the gist—terco and idea tonta, stubborn and stupid idea. They'd had problems with droughts and fires. They lost two dozen lime trees (that she'd made him transplant) to poor drainage, something he had warned her about. She stopped getting angry. She listened to him more.

Several times when he was young, he'd come late to work or even miss a day after a weekend of drinking. Fred often told her to get her house in order, or he'd do it for her. She'd lay Alejandro off for a week as punishment, not willing to train someone to replace him. She covered for him to Fred when necessary.

Once, when Fred was out of town, Alejandro showed up late at night, drunk, with a couple of buddies in the back of his pickup truck. He hadn't been bold enough to come right up to the house but parked by the barn, stood in the truck bed with his friends, and played music. She woke to the squeal of the accordion and the large strum of a guitar and tore out of the house to put a stop to it before it woke the children. She knew it would be him.

As soon as he saw her there in her nightgown, he put down his violin. They had a moment across the moonlit distance, a pause in their lives, before Lillian remembered herself and shouted, "Alejandro!"

Alejandro got down and jumped into the cab and drove off, his friends sitting in the back, awkwardly holding on to their instruments. Lillian knew she'd have to fire him, at the same time thinking of his violin and how she hadn't known he played. But he didn't come back to work. She didn't call him; she didn't know what to say. After a week, she hired someone part-time, then another when the first didn't work out. She told Fred that Alejandro had quit. She kept her efforts up in the garden but took to wearing perfume to override her anger and the scents that reminded her of Alejandro.

Three months later, Alejandro drove into the yard while she was sorting pottings in the barn. He had a young girl with him, barely twenty, small and fierce-eyed.

"Señora Walsh, this is my wife, Rosalba."

Lillian was surprised at how relieved she was to see him. She held her hand out to the girl. "Me gusta mucho conocerte." Her Spanish was rudimentary and formal.

"And nice to meet you, too," Rosalba replied in perfect English.

"Señora, I'd like to come back to work." Alejandro looked down at the hat in his hands.

"Monday," Lillian said, and that was that.

There were evolving atmospheric shifts in their relationship. Alejandro gave up drinking as far as Lillian could tell. She felt compelled to take Rosalba under her wing. Lillian bought the couple a washer and dryer for their wedding and generous gifts for the children as they came—a girl and two boys. She felt gratitude for whatever part

Rosalba played in keeping Alejandro on track. She co-signed a loan so they could buy a house. When Rosalba was still alive, she was polite and gracious but pushed back against Lillian's generosity by standing guard over her family's privacy. In time, Lillian and Alejandro settled into a casual formality. They no longer fought like siblings. There were no more lingering looks.

"Lillian." Alejandro had been fiddling with his napkin for several minutes.

Lillian felt his discomfort today. It agitated her. It was a familiar feeling from long ago. She got up and down from the table to fetch this or that. Now she poured more tea into his glass.

He held up his hand in protest. "No, no, that's enough." She reached to stack the plates. "Lillian, please sit," he said again, watching her as she started to rise from the table. "Alicia is being transferred to Sacramento," he said. Alicia had moved into Alejandro's home with her children after her divorce five years ago. Rosalba had been gone a long time now. "It's a good job she has. It's a good transfer," he said.

Lillian felt the familiar thrill of the music of his voice—the slightly odd syntax, the soft touch of the tongue on the "n." There was nothing that matched it.

He fiddled with the napkin again. "She wants me to go with her."

She laid her arm on the table next to his to see the contrast. The differences they lived, all this time, side by side. His arms were still strong, and the skin held tight to the muscular matrix beneath, unlike hers, which seemed to loosen daily. She felt someday her skin would peel in weightless tufts and fly away like dandelion heads.

She put her hand on his and said, "No." She couldn't look at him.

"I know someone who can take over for me."

She still couldn't look at him.

She said, "No," again, but barely heard her own voice. She didn't notice when he slipped his hand out from under hers.

Lillian wrote to Alejandro once a month. At first, after he'd left, she would call him several times a week with questions about his new life. When he seemed reluctant to share, she would ask for advice about this tree or that creeper. At first he was helpful, but he soon found excuses to get off the phone. He would say he was reading to Isabel, Alicia's youngest, who attended kindergarten half-day, or he was on his way to the market or a doctor's appointment. When she seemed alarmed about the doctor's appointment, he said he'd misspoken; it was really the dentist. She knew then that he was lying, that he was uncomfortable talking to her on the phone.

She started writing instead, keeping him up with any local news or how Fred was doing. Alejandro wrote her back, though not as often, telling her about the house that Alicia was buying and the garden he kept in the backyard. He was growing vegetables and teaching the children about the plants. She wrote about her grandchildren, too, although she had little hands-on experience, seeing them twice a year at most. They exchanged Christmas cards.

Genuine was unreachable when Fred had his last debilitating stroke, and Lillian knew that this, too, was the end of another chapter. She hired an agency that sent nurses in twelve-hour rotations to dress and bathe him and see to his medications. But she cooked all his soft meals and fed him herself, wiping the slack side of his mouth that he couldn't control. She had a ramp installed on the front porch and took him outside in his wheelchair every day, showing him the different plants, telling him all that she knew about a specimen's origin and when she had planted it. She enjoyed caring for him in this simple way. She felt the tenderness of the times. She never mentioned Alejandro.

After

2012 - 2013

The triple-digit heat on the day of Lars's funeral was the opening act for a record drought. It arrived suddenly, like his death, and lingered across the Midwest for the rest of the summer. The promise of rain on the day Kevin left town went unrealized. Here in Iowa, the beans turned to rust and died as the corn stood in the fields like dusty clay soldiers. The devil had come to occupy the Earth, and the heat and grief that occupied the space around us seemed as incompatible as passion to indifference. A week after Kevin left, Andrew, now my only sibling, flew back to Seattle the same day Stephanie's parents arrived to drive her home to Chicago. I was especially sad for Stephanie to have such a rug pulled out from under her life.

My grief was the catalyst that allowed me to finally close the chapter with Kevin. Having no plans, I stayed on with my parents. We roamed the house like marooned survivors waiting to be rescued and carried back to our old lives. We paid attention to the weather and made it the central theme of our conversations, the way strangers do. The heat index captivated us. We obsessed over what was happening to the beans and corn as if we were farmers. I went to work around the house like a sister wife, insisting on my share of the chores. I watered the lawn and garden until rationing was put in place: only

Tuesdays and Saturdays. Sometimes I'd sneak out in the pre-dawn hours on the wrong day to soak the vegetables. After a bit, we let the lawn go, but I was intent on saving the tomatoes. We were so fatigued by the heat that even the specter of Lars couldn't stir us. The only noise in our heads was the drone of the air conditioning.

A brief cold front in late August woke us up. Giddy with relief over the change in weather, we became more wary of each other. Polite. Cautious. We were truly stranded then, circling each other in our reborn grief, watchful of the way we might laugh at something, enjoy a meal, or find interest in something other than the weather. A quick look said it all—don't forget, we are grieving. Then, a touch on the arm—no, it's okay; it's natural.

For me, everyday tasks bore new import. Doing the laundry, washing the dishes, and slicing the tomatoes that had survived after all inspired an inner watchfulness. I was always burdened with the knowledge that life had irrevocably changed.

I've just had a conversation about shoes.

But Lars is dead.

That was a good dinner.

Lars is really dead.

There were also the unspoken things my parents must have been thinking. How could they not? As fall took hold, there was a change in our internal temperatures, too. It was the coolness of longing—for Lars, for the past, for all of those unrealized futures.

I caught my dad looking at me one late afternoon when he thought I didn't notice. It was the end of September, and the garden was done for the year. I'd been turning over the plants and applying mulch when something made me turn toward the kitchen window. He raised his hand to wave. I felt certain he'd been watching me for a while.

I peeled off my gloves and put my mother's tools back in the small shed by the garage. The back entrance to the house was through a limestone patio with handcrafted steps up to the door. I pictured them covered in ice and imagined the difficulty of shoveling the uneven stones. The door opened directly into the kitchen with no place for muddy garden shoes or snowy winter boots when the time came. The house was full of quirks: tall ceilings, impossibly small closets, nicely tiled but inconveniently placed bathrooms, and these steps, lacking normal Midwestern utility. It was not the split-level home of our youth. It was not my home at all. It belonged only to our parents.

"Everything all right?" I asked my dad, who was still gazing out the window when I came in. I hadn't expected him home from work yet.

His pale Nordic hair seemed to have lost all color. Flecks of light reflected from the overhead and bounced off its translucent ends. I guess this is what happens before the gray. He nodded, gave me a half smile, and left the room. I heard him click on the TV, so I didn't follow. My mother was out, and it was getting late. I started dinner.

I cut up some tomatoes that had been ripening on the windowsill and made a salad and some chicken. I got the table ready and waited, reluctant to sit and eat alone with my dad. There was a hazy disturbance developing in our relationship. My mother came home just in time with the right amount of cheerfulness—enough to raise the barometer but not too much to let us forget.

There were shifting plates of tension in the house. My mother and I were getting closer; my dad and I seemed to be gaining distance. Though my dad is a reserved man, true to his genetic disposition, he and I have always been of the same mind. Since Lars, he avoids looking me in the eye. I realized now that when he'd said to me at the hospital, "I'm so glad we have you," he wasn't talking about me, his daughter, but about my healing abilities. My mother said I was wrong, but I remain unconvinced.

Kevin tried to come visit, but I told him no.

"My new job starts in two weeks," he said. "I could come now, and we could spend some time together." He had been at our house in Boone but was taking a job in New York.

"I can't," I said and held the phone in front of me, so I could pretend I was telling him this to his face.

"I miss Lars, too," he said.

I had been ignoring this nagging little fact. Fifteen years is a marriage, no matter the legalities. He had been a part of our family.

"I know," I said. "I don't think they're ready for company," I lied.

A week later, we settled our finances with only minor difficulty, though there was no quick way to sell the house. The market had become so bad. Still, I'll have enough to live on for a couple of years if I'm careful, and Kevin will have a good start in New York. We leased the house to Arliss for the expenses for two years. She and Rusty will run it as a B&B, and I'm happy knowing she'll take care of it.

"I'd like to stay a while longer," I said to my mother.

We were in the kitchen. It was late October, and Andrew was coming for Thanksgiving. I wanted to see him, and more than that, I knew I couldn't face anything other than the flat expanse of the Midwest. I didn't want sun; I didn't want the particular beauty of the mountains. I couldn't imagine cheery California.

"Of course," my mother said.

I'd noticed she'd been managing to get herself out of the house as much as possible during the week. She had taught a class or two per semester for years, first at our school, then at the community college. She quit when Lars finished college, though she volunteered at the museum twice a month. Now she spent time at the library, volunteered extra hours at the museum whenever they called her, and met with friends for coffee. She had a small studio next to the garage, and she often spent time puttering around in there, though I hadn't seen any paintings. She talked about going back to work in January.

"Are you sure I'm not in the way?"

The story of my mother and me is tangled in so many ways. Religion, healing, the tension I created in her relationship with my father. We've been combing it out with small gestures these last months.

"Of course you're not in the way," she said and reached to stroke my hair, something she did when I was a child, as if stroking my hair was the key to calming my insides.

The weekends were a little awkward with both parents fussing over how they might entertain me, conjuring activities for the three of us. I imagined they also discussed what they'd like to do if I weren't there. I'd tell them I had plans. Surprisingly, they didn't probe. I would take one of their cars and drive around old neighborhoods, places where I might have visited friends in my youth. I had no friends to visit now.

I drove the ten miles to St. Timothy's at least once a weekend, if not more, sometimes parking across the street from the church, sometimes in the parking lot. I never went in. I saw Father Hanson walking from his car to the rectory a few times. He never looked my way. Then one day as I was listening to some old nineties music in the car, engine running in the cold, there was a loud rap next to my head. It startled me, but not as much as staring up into Father Hanson's face through the winter dirt of the car window. Before I had a chance to respond, he placed his flat palm on the window for a few seconds, shook his head, then turned and walked away. But no, that didn't happen. That scene came to me in a dream and stayed in my thoughts, disturbingly, for weeks.

On days when I was alone in the house, I would sit in various rooms, often for hours, reading or daydreaming—imagining what life would have been like if we'd grown up here, and what holidays might be like with a houseful of grandchildren. It would happen someday with Andrew, but I couldn't see an inch of my own future.

The house's attic, small and barely tall enough for me to stand, was astonishingly tidy, each childhood reduced to a green bin with a name. Typical things like report cards, a sampling of drawings, and baby journals. When had my mother filled out baby journals? I found

Barbie and Ken in my bin, naked and child-stained. Barbie's hair was matted. I don't remember having them. It seems like something my mother would never have allowed. I didn't ask. One evening in early November, I brought Lars's bin downstairs and spread his things around. It threw my parents off-kilter. I was dredging it up again, the loss to be looked at, examined, remembered. But of course, we were remembering still—every day.

At Thanksgiving, the house became somewhat cheery. Stephanie, who called my mother every Saturday morning, also came for the holiday. Her sweet face and the startling way she talked about Lars buoyed us. She brought some videos Lars had made of comedy routines he'd been working on. And one—she brought copies for each of us—that he'd made just for the family. It was a hilarious routine of Lars in a long black wig channeling me at my worst. He called himself "The Magic Hair" and waved the braid about in benediction to the camera. We laughed and cried the whole weekend.

I stayed. Stephanie came back for Christmas, but it wasn't the same. Andrew couldn't get leave from work, and Stephanie had lost her good humor. Everyone strived. It was unseasonably warm. It missed the mark of our expectations.

One day, after Christmas, my mother told me that Kevin had called. We were sitting at the kitchen table. She was having some afternoon tea, and I was peeling potatoes for dinner. I was doing all the cooking now.

"I'll call him back after dinner."

"No." She paused. "He called to talk to me."

I took the bowl of potatoes over to the sink to wash.

"He sounded lonely."

"Mom, I can't . . ."

"Okay," she said.

It had taken years for my mother to warm up to Kevin, unlike my dad. The age difference didn't help, but she eventually became as fond of him as she dared. She sensed the impermanence and tried, in her way, to make it up to Kevin by including him in the family fold. I never shared our troubles or my doubts. I wasn't yet ready to explain that until these past months, I had not had a truly unstructured day since I'd met Kevin. Despite the breathless grief, there was a tiny turbine of freedom building in my chest.

"Thanks for the braids," I said. I needed to change the subject.

That morning I'd found a faded manila envelope in my room. It contained the two braids some boy had cut off when I was in kindergarten.

"I'd forgotten they were different lengths."

"I had to trim off so much of the rest of your hair to get it even," she said as she stared into her tea. And then, "Lars wasn't your fault."

She had said this before, many times, but I am a selfish person. I need to be the owner of the guilt. I'd spent months going over every healing that had ever failed and every activity that preceded that failure.

"You can't know that. Maybe if I hadn't healed that man before I left the house . . ."

"I know this," she said. "A mother tries to protect a child from every harm, but it's really a game she plays with fate. Don't play games with yourself, Gen. Your brother was riding a motorcycle that your father encouraged him to buy. There are so many ways in which we all can feel guilty. I'm telling you not to."

"I'm so sorry," I said and thought of pretty Stephanie weeping at the funeral. There was no comely weeping for me, only an ugly release of guttural sobs and the peppery burn of overdue tears. All that I held myself accountable for seemed nothing next to the pile that was the absence of Lars. Guilt and blame could not repair the loss.

In January, the temperature dropped like an elevator cut loose in its shaft. Ice storms knocked down trees and power lines twice that month and three times in February. In March, I told my parents I was leaving.

"Where will you go?" My mother's voice betrayed a combination of concern and slight relief. Before I could answer she said, "You don't need to go. I worry—your dad and I both worry. We've never seen you so restless."

I was restless, and itchy, but I couldn't talk about it. It was the elephant in the house that was my body, blundering through my veins, sitting on my mind, kicking at my heart. I was in withdrawal. And not just from those I'd loved. I was in withdrawal from healing. The energy that runs through me when I heal someone is what I imagine a cocaine user feels on the first try. Kevin had suspected this. It had lain between us like a not-so-secret lover, the wedge that splintered under his skin and drove him mad. It was not the babies or the lack of them; it was not the question of marriage, or money, or any such quotidian cause of our demise. So here I am, doing the very thing he pleaded with me to do, but doing it for myself for some sense of atonement. Not healing is my flagellant.

"You need to start healing people again," my mother said. I was surprised that she would guess.

"I need to find someone like me."

Over the years, I had heard of so many healers. Some claimed to be "energy" healers; others claimed to heal by prayer. There were supposedly healers from Native American tribes, Russia, and South America. I'd never met one who could do what I do.

"You've always claimed there wasn't anyone," my mother said.

"I don't think Kevin really wanted me to find someone." As I said it, I realized the truth of it for the first time.

I'd been scouring the Internet in recent weeks, something I'd always left to Kevin. There are hundreds of websites—so many claims, so many disclaimers. But there are some that look promising. I need to meet some of these healers. I need to see for myself. One of them might be exactly like me. One of them might be genuine.

"Your father and I looked when you were young. We wrote to people and other parents. Nothing ever materialized."

I think I knew this but had forgotten, as if parts of my life had been boxed up like the keepsake bins.

"It must have been hard for you." I've said all this before.

"It was always complicated. It was never hard." She reached out for my head.

I leaned into her. I need this, too, this stroke of her love. I will always need this.

Acknowledgements
2018

Writing requires both solitude and connection. I am sincerely grateful to the large community of readers, writers, friends, and family who encouraged, taught, read, reviewed, and urged me in my efforts.

With deep appreciation to:

Meghan Daum, Al Davis, and all the members of the Fairfield Book Prize Committee who chose The Genuine Stories for this remarkable honor.

Nayt Rundquist, Kevin Carollo, Travis Dolence, and their band of dedicated students at New Rivers Press, who shepherded the work to publication. In particular, I'd like to thank Olivia Carlson, Mia Duncan, Laura Grimm, Cameron Schulz, April Schwandt, and Hope Pauly.

The faculty of the Fairfield University MFA in Creative Writing Program who mentored me, encouraged me, and believed in my writing, with a special shout out to MFA Founder, Michael C. White, who brought us all together and to Elisabeth Hastings, who kept us happy on our island home.

Eugenia Kim, Karen Osborn, and Nalini Jones who read, re-read, and re-read some more and guided me with the particular kindness that is friendship.

Wayne Johnson, my first mentor, who taught me so much about writing and was the first one to meet Genuine on the page.

My many dear friends and family members who read early drafts, offered feedback, and supported my efforts the way dear friends do.

My husband Bob, for always being my biggest fan, and to our children, Genevra, Ben, and Chétana, for teaching me about motherhood and its intersection with the greater world.

About the Author
2018

Susan Smith Daniels is a 2012 graduate of Fairfield University's MFA program. She was awarded the FUMFA Book Prize for this collection of stories. She resides with her family in Iowa and is currently working on her PhD in Creative Writing at Bath Spa University. She is the author of *The Horse Show Mom's Survival Guide*, The Lyons Press, 2005.

About
New Rivers Press

New Rivers Press emerged from a drafty Massachusetts barn in winter 1968. Intent on publishing work by new and emerging poets, founder C.W. "Bill" Truesdale labored for weeks over an old Chandler & Price letterpress to publish three hundred fifty copies of Margaret Randall's collection So Many Rooms Has a House but One Roof. About four hundred titles later, New Rivers is now a nonprofit learning press, based since 2001 at Minnesota State University Moorhead. Charles Baxter, one of the first authors with New Rivers calls the press "the hidden backbone of the American literary tradition."

As a learning press, New Rivers guides student editors, designers, writers, and filmmakers through the various processes involved in selecting, editing, designing, publishing, and distributing literary books. In working, learning, and interning with New Rivers Press, students gain integral real-world knowledge that they bring with them into the publishing workforce at positions with publishers across the country, or to begin their own small presses and literary magazines.

Please visit our website: newriverspress.com for more information.